Mystery of Lost Canyon

Also by Gordon D. Shirreffs

Mystery of Lost Canyon

Gordon D. Shirreffs

WOLFPACK
PUBLISHING
— EST 2013 —

Mystery of Lost Canyon
Paperback Edition
Copyright © 2024 (As Revised) Gordon D. Shirreffs

Wolfpack Publishing
701 S. Howard Ave. 106-324
Tampa, Florida 33609

wolfpackpublishing.com

Paperback ISBN 978-1-63977-590-3
eBook ISBN 978-1-63977-990-1

To John W. Starnes, who helped me as he helped so many others.

Mystery of Lost Canyon

Chapter 1

Huntress Returns to Lake Mead

THE OUTBOARD MOTORBOAT SLID EASILY FROM the tilt trailer into the shallow waters of Lake Mead as Jerry Hunter reeled out the nylon winch line. When the boat was fully afloat, little Whitey Cramer waded to the bow and unsnapped the line from the bow eyelet. Jerry quickly reeled in the line and waved a hand to big Buck Lyon who was watching the launching from the driver's seat of his battered pickup truck. Buck drove the truck forward until the trailer was out of the water, then began to carry supplies and equipment from the truck to the boat.

Jerry stood in the shallow water looking at the eighteen-foot boat. It had been a long time since she had been afloat. In fact, he had never expected to see her in the water again. She had been gathering dust in the Hunter garage for almost three years until Jerry's mother, seeing the look in Jerry's eyes, had managed to convince her husband that it served no purpose to let such a fine boat slowly rot away because of sentimental attachment. Whether it was her plea, or Bill Hunter's love of a good boat that had turned the tide, he had agreed to let Jerry and his two close friends, Whitey and Buck, take over the boat on the condition that they would keep her up and pay all expenses. That had been less than a month ago, and in that time the boat had been cleaned, repainted, furbished from stem to stern and fitted with an excellent secondhand fifty-horsepower, manual starting, outboard motor, to replace the old thirty-five horsepower motor that had been gathering dust along with the boat for the past years.

Buck Lyon stopped beside Jerry. "I never expected to see her afloat in my lifetime," he said quietly.

"It's where she belongs," said Jerry. "Uncle Chuck would have wanted it that way."

Buck nodded. He waded out and began to store gear in the wide cockpit of the boat. "Better get going," he said. "We'll want to be beyond Boulder Canyon before it gets too dark."

Whitey Cramer slapped the side of the boat. "She's a dream, men! We ought to give her a name though."

Buck waded back to the shore and looked at the boat. "I think we ought to call her *Huntress*," he said., "Not only because of the name of the men who built her but also because of her mission."

Whitey nodded. "I like it! I like it!"

Jerry walked up to the truck. "Suits me," he said. He drove the truck into the parking lot and wound up the cracked windows. The truck had seen far better days, but she served her purpose well enough. Time and time again, the three friends had driven that truck far into the canyons that led down to the waters of Lake Mead in their searching. Now, to further the hunt, they had a boat that could carry them on the lake itself.

Down at the water's edge the big outboard motor

kicked over, spluttered, then died. Again, she kicked over, throbbed erratically, then settled down to business. Jerry waded out and turned the bow of the boat until it pointed toward the open lake. He climbed into the spacious cockpit where Whitey was racking the fishing rods against the port side.

"Take her out, Jerry," said Buck.

Jerry shrugged. "It doesn't matter who takes her out," he said. He was quite sure he sounded convincing.

The two of them looked at him and he knew well enough what was on their minds. Although the three of them would share the boat and its adventures, it still had been built mostly by the skilled and loving hands of Chuck Hunter, Jerry's uncle. The last time it had been out on the lake, Chuck had taken Jerry with him on a marvelous seven-day expedition into the little-known areas of the lake. After that trip the boat swung at anchor at the marina for months, unused and forlorn, until at last Bill Hunter had sent Jerry and his two friends down to get it and bring it up to the Hunter home in Boulder City. That had been three years ago.

Jerry dropped into the seat and took the wheel, moving the boat out into the deeper water at slow speed, past the bobbing moored boats. An incoming boat passed them, and the driver waved at Jerry. "It's getting a little sloppy out there," he called.

The bright desert sun glinted from the metallic blue waters. Now and then a whitecap reared up, then vanished from sight. Mead could kick up a fuss in a hurry at times, but the red storm warning flags were not flying as yet. The boys would be well up the lake before it got too rough. *Huntress* was rugged and seaworthy enough in any case. Chuck Hunter had built her of plywood, fastened with bronze nails, screws and bolts, then had covered her with Fiberglas. It had been Bill Hunter who had suggested to the boys that they add extra flotation by the use of Styrofoam blocks, as well as flowing liquid Styrofoam into the bilges and any other place they could find. Even if she were swamped, she'd stay afloat and keep her crew afloat as well.

They were well out from the marina when Whitey dropped into the seat beside Jerry and rested a hand on the wheel. He handed Jerry the field glasses. "I'll steer while you take a look along the road, right at the far side of the parking lot," he said quietly.

Jerry turned and raised the glasses, focusing them on the road. A big sedan was parked there, and a tall man was standing beside it looking toward the lake. His face seemed to swim into view in the powerful glasses. It was Jerry's father. As far as Jerry knew, his father was supposed to be in Las Vegas that day on business. Jerry handed the glasses back to Whitey.

"Who is it?" asked Buck.

"My father," said Jerry.

There was no need to say more. The boat and Jerry's father and uncle had been firmly joined together in the years before Jerry's uncle had vanished somewhere on the lake, or near it, supposedly drowned during a vicious windstorm that had lashed the lake into a frenzy. Bill Hunter had never gone out on the lake again, although before the tragedy, he had spent many weekends exploring and fishing on the lake with his brother and Jerry.

"Well, all I have to say," said Whitey, "is that your father really thinks we're going bass fishing, Jerry."

Buck stowed away a sleeping bag. "I think we all know Mister Hunter better than that," he said.

"He say anything at all to you?" asked Whitey of Jerry.

Jerry gave the motor more throttle. She was beginning to plane a little as she gained speed. "All he said was that he didn't expect my grades to go down. If I don't get out of school with good enough grades to get into college in the fall, you can bet your bottom dollar this boat will end up in the garage again."

"Perish forbid!" said Whitey.

Jerry gave her still more throttle and she began to move *like* a thing alive, eager for open water after years of inactivity. She bounced a little, throwing up silvery sheets of spray to either side of the bow.

Buck grinned. "We didn't make a mistake getting this fifty-horse job," he said. He patted the throbbing motor. "She hums like a jet!"

The wide V wake creamed out behind the speeding boat in sharp contrast to the almost vitriolic blue color of the water. The flying spray glittered like diamonds in the bright desert sunlight, as though some wanton hand were scattering the precious gems pell-mell across the water. *Huntress* dipped into the wake of a large inboard cruiser, surged down, then flung herself up the far rise like an Irving thing. She came down lightly on her bottom, spanking the waves, then cut a furrow through the water with an easy motion.

Whitey Cramer looked at Jerry. "She's actually frolicking, Jerry," he said in an awed voice.

Buck nodded. "Maybe she knows why we've taken her over," he said quietly. *"She knows…"*

They passed the sleeping lump of Sentinel Island and Jerry set a course that would take them in a straight line to Beacon Island.

"And you were worried about us not getting beyond

Boulder Canyon before dusk," said Whitey to Buck. "We can camp well beyond Boulder Canyon at this rate of speed."

Jerry eased the throttle a little, feeling the response of the boat until he found her easiest cruising speed. He felt at home again. There are some people who have such a feeling in a car, or plane, or on the back of a good saddle horse, but to the born boatman, there is nothing quite as satisfying and exhilarating as being out on open water in a good, well-powered boat, with two good companions and two whole days ahead of them with nothing to do but fish, swim, and explore. It was the exploring that appealed most to him. He had never bought the idea that Uncle Chuck had been lost on the lake. Though he had been alone in a smaller and less powerful boat, it wasn't like him to take unnecessary chances on the lake at night in bad weather. It just wasn't him! Somewhere, in the mazes of the great lake, in one of the coves or bays, that in times past had been valleys and canyons, in a country that had been one of the driest parts of the southwest since before the time of man and now was a huge manmade lake one hundred and fifteen miles long and hundreds of feet deep, there would be a clue to the mysterious disappearance of Charles Hunter. There *had* to be!

Whitey and Buck stowed the rest of the gear. Up forward, below the foredeck, were two bunks covered with pads, upon which Jerry and Buck, as the biggest of the trio, would sleep, while Whitey, who tipped the scales at a mean one hundred and thirty pounds, soaking wet, would sleep in the wide cockpit, all five feet six inches of him. There had been some powerful arguments advanced by Whitey and lost, despite the fact he had tried to carry the argument by claiming his brain weight was double that of his two bigger companions put together. The final decision had been made by Buck Lyon, all one hundred and eighty pounds of him, well distributed on an even six feet of frame, who had quietly told Whitey that if he wanted to pit his brain against Buck's brawn, no holds barred, he could have Buck's bunk. So Whitey had been quartered in the cockpit, claiming, of course, that the fresh air was more to his liking.

The sun beat down on the incredible metallic blue of the water, in marked contrast to the sharp color-stained hills that gripped the great lake in their widespread arms. Along the bases of the hills and mountains, where they met the sheer blue waters of the lake, were wide bands of lighter color, showing the full depth of the lake at times in a natural marker. There was another great contrast. The vast body of water, over five hundred feet deep in places, was encircled by the towering, fantastically colored hills, as dry as prehistoric bones. This had been desert and mountain country for eons and even though man had made a great reservoir of the precious fluid right in the very heart of waterless country, it seemed to Jerry Hunter that the desert and mountains had not given up the age-old fight altogether. It was as if they were watching and waiting, quietly and unobtrusively. Always...watching and waiting for their chance...

High to the right, towering thousands of feet above the lake, was the flat-topped mass of Fortification Mountain, a huge pile of dark volcanic rock. While on the lower slopes, the gay coloring of the Paint Pots seemed to drift down to meet the cobalt blue of the lake shore.

At such times, viewing the immensity of the land about the lake, Jerry Hunter's heart would sink within him. How was it possible, in this great land, to find a man who had been lost without trace for over three years?

"If there's a clue in these mountains, or along the lake, Jerry," said Whitey, "we'll find it this trip, or keep coming back until we do find one."

Jerry glanced quickly at the younger boy. He was seventeen, a year younger than both Buck and Jerry, but in some ways, he was the most mature of the three of them. He had an uncanny knack of reading people's minds. He hadn't lettered in football as Buck had done, nor in track as Jerry had done, but he had never missed the honor roll in his high school years, and although he was only seventeen, he was graduating in June with his two friends.

Although it was only May, already the torrid heat of summer was present in the Lake Mead country. The mountains and canyons beyond the lake, in the arid and isolated country to the north, east, and south, became suburbs of hell itself from May well on until November. There were many forgotten trails in those mountains; abandoned mines; ghost towns, although few in number; Indian village sites, almost impossible to find. Many men had wandered into that country and had vanished forever, or perhaps their bones marked their final stopping place. Jerry Hunter could not bring himself to believe that his uncle's skeleton marked a last stopping place, nor could he believe it was buried beneath the waters of Lake Mead.

Maybe *Huntress* would help the three boys more than the truck had, for the old pickup was limited to the roads, some of them hardly more than rutted trails through the harsh, inhospitable country. They had taken the truck down many of the old washes that met the lake, and had explored from there, but it had become hopeless after six months of trial. *Huntress* could poke into the coves and bays, the nooks and crannies of five hundred and fifty miles of shoreline, the bottoms of the now water-filled canyons, and take them to the mouths of the dry canyons that debouched to meet the lake and river. There would be plenty of footwork though.

"Maybe we could trade this thing in for a helicopter," said Whitey as he opened a king-sized Coke and handed it to Jerry.

Jerry glanced at him again. The thought had occurred to Jerry many times a hopeless, yet intriguing thought.

Buck accepted a Coke from Whitey and sat down on a sleeping bag. "Sure could swoop down into these canyons with that. Chase jack rabbits and coyotes. Yieee!"

"Listen to him!" said Whitey.

"Maybe a submarine would do better," said Jerry.

"You don't really believe he drowned, do you, Jerry?" asked Whitey.

"His boat was pretty small," said Jerry.

"Why didn't he take *Huntress*?"

"Dad wanted to use it that weekend. We had relatives coming in from LA for the fishing. Uncle Chuck had his other boat. It was an aluminum job with a twenty-horse-power motor. It wasn't decked, but it had flotation tanks under the seats and was pretty seaworthy, even if it was only fourteen feet long. He used it quite a bit. Called it *Explorer*."

"I remember it," said Buck. "Nice little boat. No speed. But it was a fine boat for fishing and poking about in. They never found a trace of it, did they?"

Jerry shook his head. They were rounding Burro Point. The sun was slanting down in the west. "He was beyond Boulder Canyon," he said quietly. "That we know, because he was seen there the day before he disappeared, heading east."

"Big help," said Whitey. He sipped his drink. "He could have gone north up Overton Arm, or south to Bonelli Landing, or maybe Detrital Wash."

Buck nodded. "Or around East Point toward the Virgin Canyon area. There's an awful lot of country beyond East Point up the river toward Iceberg Canyon." He whistled softly.

Jerry looked back at them. "We've combed the country pretty well around Bonelli Landing, Detrital Wash, and Temple Bar Landing. No use putting in there."

"So?" said Whitey.

"I'd like to try along all those coves and bays from Detrital Wash clear around East Point to Temple Bar Landing."

"There's a lot of them," said Whitey gloomily.

Buck poured the last mouthful of his Coke over Whitey's ashy blonde hair and rubbed it in briskly with a large paw of a hand. "What *else* we got to do, Whitey, old squid?" he said with a wide grin on his face.

Jerry looked ahead. "Whitey is right," he said.

Buck stood up and let the breeze flow about him. "Well, we can start with the first one and keep going until we try them all, Jerry. You know, I think we're going to have some luck this trip. We've had too many dry runs. Our luck has to change."

"Amen," said Whitey.

They passed Beacon Island, leaving the Lower Basin, then entered Boulder Canyon, threading through the narrower waters until they entered the roughly triangular shaped area of Virgin Basin, the area where Chuck Hunter had last been seen. They crossed the basin on a southeasterly course toward the huge, humped mass of land that thrust itself out into the basin to terminate in East Point. From Detrital Wash, deep in a large cove, to East Point, thence south again to Temple Bar Landing was a good thirteen to fifteen miles, not counting the extent of the many indentations into the land mass, which would add considerably to the mileage, but as Buck had said ungrammatically, "What *else* we got to do, Whitey, old squid?"

It was dusk when they eased into the landing at Detrital Wash and cut the engine. The boat grounded with a grating noise. After the steady humming of the engine for twenty-five watery miles, the sudden quiet seemed to descend like a curtain over the wash. There wasn't a soul in sight. The sun was gone, and it began to grow cool in the darkness.

The boys, all experienced campers, worked quickly and efficiently to set up their simple camp. Whitey started the gas stove and began the meal while Buck gathered driftwood for a campfire. Jerry unrolled the sleeping bags and wedged up the side of the boat so that it was level for sleeping purposes, then he put up the navy type canvas top to provide shelter from the cold night winds that sometimes swept through the water-filled canyons and basins.

When they had finished eating and cleaned the dishes, they sat about the campfire and sipped their coffee. The wind shifted and rustled the scant dry brush and scrub trees.

"Just what was Chuck Hunter looking for around here?" asked Whitey.

"I heard it was uranium," said Buck. He looked at Jerry. "Wasn't he a mining engineer, Jerry?"

"No," said Jerry. "He had studied geology in college and took an interest in it. My father was always sorry that Uncle Chuck hadn't gone on to become an engineer as he had done. Uncle Chuck was interested in geology, but then he was interested in many things. He made his living by photography and writing travel articles.

"That's why he was always poking about in the back canyons then?" said Whitey. "I heard he was looking for old Indian relics. There's supposed to be a lost cliff dwelling or something like that in one of these canyons. Probably under water by now like some of those up Overton Arm."

Jerry leaned back against a rock and looked toward the dark waters of the lake. "He had a collection of Indian relics, and pioneer relics, *and* war relics, from his war service. He also collected guns, bows, swords, and anything else he could get his hands on."

"How about salt and pepper shakers?" said Whitey.

Buck clamped a huge hand over Whitey's mouth. "Go on, Jerry," he said, ignoring Whitey's struggles.

Jerry leaned closer to the two of them and lowered his voice, although there couldn't possibly be anyone within hearing distance of them in that remote spot "I don't think it was uranium, or relics, or lost mines, or anything like that."

"Why do you say so?" asked Buck.

"He had some old maps that were made of this area in the time before and after the Civil War. That was when the Colorado was first traversed by men. Major John Powell came through here about 1869, as far as I can recollect. On Powell's second trip he explored many of the side canyons. Uncle Chuck had a copy of one of Powell's books, and copies of some of his maps. I used to look at them now and then, but there wasn't any treasure or anything like that marked on them."

"Maybe you didn't recognize treasure markings on the maps," said Whitey.

Jerry shook his head. "There weren't any. You know, Uncle Chuck had an amazing memory, almost photographic, I'd say. He could remember trails and landmarks and things like that better than anyone I ever knew. If he did have a map with clues to a treasure, he'd likely memorize any markings in case someone else might get a look at them if he had written them down."

"Then why?" asked Buck. He looked up at the dark masses of rocks topped by the dark blue of the night sky, stippled with a myriad ice chip star.

Jerry stood up. "I don't know. I don't care *why* he came in here. I just want to find him or find his body." He walked to the boat.

Whitey looked at Buck and shrugged. They put out the fire and walked to the boat. Jerry and Buck crawled into their bunks and Whitey made himself comfortable in the cockpit. The water lapped gently against the sides of the *Huntress* and the dry wind whispered softly through the dark canyons. Now and then a fish broke water. Far across the sleeping hills came the mournful cry of a coyote.

Chapter 2

Strangers in the Night

A HAND CLOSED OVER JERRY'S MOUTH. HE opened his eyes to look up into the dim face of Whitey Cramer. Whitey put his mouth close to Jerry's right ear. "I think I heard voices out on the water," he said softly. He took his hand from Jerry's mouth.

"So?" said Jerry. He rose on an elbow, careful not to crack his head against the deck above him. "Fishermen, maybe?"

"It's after midnight," said Whitey.

"Sometimes you get a little too dramatic," growled Jerry. He crawled out of his bunk into the cockpit. It was as dark as the inside of a boot out in the cove. Water and land fused together in common darkness, with the sky hardly much lighter. A cool wind blew from the wash. The water lapped against the side of the boat and onto the shingle where the wash met the water.

Jerry peered out into the cove until his eyes ached. "You and your imagination," he said.

"What's going on there?" hissed Buck.

Jerry shrugged. "Keep it low," he said. "Doctor Watson here thinks he heard voices out there."

"Mermaids, maybe," Buck said sourly. He crawled out beside them.

The wind shifted. Jerry raised his head. The faint sound of voices came to him. He looked quickly at Whitey. Whitey nodded.

The three of them waited. Then they heard an unmistakable sound. That of a paddle being dropped into the bottom of a boat. It boomed faintly, then faded away, echoing faintly along the sides of the wash. It grew quiet again.

Jerry wet his dry lips. Something was strange about the whole thing. There were no lights to be seen. The lake was thick in darkness, hardly the time for someone to be blundering around in a boat without lights. The Coast Guard patrolled the area and anyone who boated on the lake without running lights after dark would be heavily fined.

Then he thought he saw something faintly outlined in the darkness. He could make out the vague silhouette of a boat. Water rippled and dripped, and he saw a man standing in the bow of the boat paddling directly toward the *Huntress*. A few more minutes of paddling and the strange boat would collide with Jerry's boat.

"What do we do?" whispered Whitey.

"Better call out and let them know we're here," said Buck in a low voice.

"Wait," said Jerry. Something was warning him— some sixth sense for which he could not account.

The boat was closer now, and three men could be seen in it—one of them paddling and the other two pushing oars against the bottom. "Where's the shore?"

said one of them. "Can't see a blasted thing in here, Mac."

"Ain't far ahead," said the man in the bow.

"You think them kids are in here?"

Cold sweat worked down Jerry's sides.

"Maybe it's the Coast Guard," whispered Whitey.

Jerry shook his head.

"Maybe they went around East Point?" said one of the men in the cockpit.

"No," said the man in the bow. "They were heading this way when our motors conked out. They're around here somewhere."

"Yeh," snarled one of the two in the cockpit. "We was going to tail them all the way from the marina. I thought you said tin's boat could outrun that Hunter kid's boat."

"It can!" rasped the man in the bow. "Musta been water in our gas or something."

"Or something," jeered the other.

"I don't like this," said Buck. He picked up the camp axe.

Jerry wiped the cold sweat from his face. Those three characters were up to no good. Why would they want to tail *Huntress* all the way from the marina?

The boat was only fifty feet away by now. Whitey picked up a paddle. Buck looked at Jerry. Jerry held up a hand.

The boat moved closer. There was no time to get their own motor started and clear out of the cove. It was time for a bluff. Jerry cupped his hands about his mouth. "Hey, you!" he yelled. "Get that scow outta here or we start shooting!"

There was a moment's hesitation. A paddle was dropped into the water. The bow of the strange boat swung around, pointing toward the mouth of the cove. A moment later someone punched electric starter buttons, and a pair of powerful outboards roared into life. The boat vanished in the thick darkness and the roaring of its motors echoed and re-echoed from the hills on each side of the cove, until they died away, and then the boys heard only the distant humming of the motors and the washing of the wake waves against the shore and the side of *Huntress*.

"What do we do now?" asked Whitey.

"We can stay here and keep on guard until daylight," said Jerry, "or get out of here right now."

"I'm not in the mood to go prowling about out there with no lights," said Buck.

"You scared?" said Whitey.

Buck hefted the axe. "Not with this in my hand."

"Won't do much good if they have guns," said Whitey.

The two older boys looked at him. "What makes you think they might have guns?" they asked together.

Whitey shrugged. "I don't think they planned to make a social call," he said.

"Wonder what they wanted?" said Buck.

————

JERRY LOOKED out into the darkness of the cove. The sound of the motors had stopped, either because they were drifting out there, or perhaps were beyond earshot. If they had gone beyond earshot, they had terrifically powerful motors indeed. An uneasy feeling came over him. Maybe they were sneak thieves. He shook his head. They were after something else.

"What do you think your uncle was actually looking for?" asked Whitey in a very, very, small voice.

"I have no idea," said Jerry.

"Maybe *they* do," said Whitey.

The three of them looked at each other, their faces taut in the dimness. "Did any of you get a good look at them?" asked Jerry.

"No," said Whitey.

Buck shook his head. "I couldn't even make out the boat other than a vague shape, or the kind of motors they had."

"Great," said Jerry dryly. "With dozens of boats on this lake, all we know is that three characters, whom we don't know, or couldn't identify, in a boat we can't recognize, are tailing us for some reason or another."

"We can't tell the Coast Guard either," said Whitey. "With the description we could give them they'd laugh us clean off the lake."

"One of them was named Mac," said Buck.

"Big deal," said Whitey. "During the war just about everybody called everybody else Mac. I do it myself."

"We can always go back home," said Jerry.

"Not on your life," said Buck. "I don't scare that easy."

"Hear, hear," said Whitey. "Ol' Fearless Lyon roars his defiance to the night and the dangers withal."

"Sometimes I wish you spoke English," said Buck.

"Who'd understand it around here outside of Jerry?" retorted Whitey.

Jerry threw up his hands in despair. "Quiet!" he snapped. "The only thing we can do is to keep guard. If the guard hears them coming back, we can leave the boat and head up the wash. If they want the boat, they can have it. What can they do with it anyway but strip it? The Coast Guard would sure pick them up in a hurry."

"They aren't interested in stripping this boat and you darn well know it," said Whitey quietly.

"Yeh," said Buck. "You guys get some sleep. I'll keep guard."

"One-hour shifts," said Jerry.

Jerry and Whitey crawled into the cramped little cabin. Jerry tried to sleep but found it impossible. Maybe it was the coffee he had been drinking after dinner. Maybe it was the crawling fear brought on by those three strangers in that mysterious boat.

Jerry closed his eyes, listening to the quiet lapping of the water in the cove.

"Jerry?" said Whitey.

"Yes?"

"Maybe we don't know what your uncle Chuck was looking for. But they do."

"You said that already."

Whitey got up on an elbow. "Yeh, but they don't know where he went either."

"So?"

"That's why they're following us. They evidently knew *Huntress* had been sitting on dry land for three years, then all of a sudden she's on the water again, all fitted out, with a better motor. Maybe they think we know what happened to your uncle and know what he found. If he did find what he was looking for, I'll bet my bottom dollar those three galoots think we know about it and are looking for it."

Jerry opened his eyes and stared up at the dark bottom surface of the deck. "All I want to do is find my uncle," he said.

"You said more than a few times that you didn't believe he was really dead."

"I don't think he is."

"Maybe they know more about his disappearance than we do. Maybe they've been waiting around for a chance to see what we aimed to do after we fixed up *Huntress.*"

"For three years, Whitey? You feeling all right in the head?"

"Yes! Maybe there's something they want that's been worth three years of their time. Something big, Jerry!"

"There goes that wildcat imagination again! Maybe Uncle Chuck found the Seven Cities of Cibola too."

Whitey lay flat. "Mark my words," he said, "we haven't seen the last of those three characters. *You can just bet that as long as we keep looking for your uncle, they'll be tailing after us.*"

Jerry did not answer. Whitey had a neat knack of forecasting the future. His imagination was based on sheer intuition as he had proved too many times to make it pure chance.

Jerry had the last watch. The dead man's watch, he thought eerily. The one before the dawn when the night seems blackest and a man's morale and physical being are at their lowest ebb. Both his uncle and his father had served in World War II, and Charles Hunter had also served in Korea. They had both told him about the predawn watch. Now he knew exactly what they had experienced.

Each faint sound of the night seemed magnified out of all proportion. A nocturnal animal scrabbled across the dry earth of the wash. A mouse squeaked. Once an owl floated over the boat on velvety wings in its silent and deadly hunt for food. A piece of driftwood bumped against the side of the boat. The wind scraped scrub tree branches against each other, and the voice of the wind itself seemed to carry small, insistent warnings of unseen danger.

Cold sweat greased the handle of the axe as Jerry held it in his lap. He was cold himself, and the blanket he had draped around his shoulders hardly held off the night chill. He wished the sun would appear more to drive away the demons of the night than the coldness of it.

There was a faint suggestion of pewter light in the eastern sky as the false dawn slowly traveled across the high mountain ranges. The canyons and valleys were still enveloped in thick velvety darkness. There wasn't a trace of light in the cove.

Jerry stood up and looked up the wash. He could barely make out the width of it, stippled with brush and scrub trees, vague and unreal in the dimness. He turned to look toward the lake and as he did so his right eye caught a flickering of light up the wash and on the side of a hill that formed one side of the depression. He turned back again. The light had vanished.

Jerry was seeing things. He rubbed his tired eyes. The light from the coming dawn was filtering through the gaps in the distant mountain range. Minutes ticked past and then, just as he was about to forget he had seen anything out of the ordinary, he saw the quick glowing of light. This time he saw the dim outline of a face behind the light, and he knew there was a man up there, smoking and watching the boat down in the cove. Then the light flicked away and, as the dawn flowed down into the wide wash, there was nothing to see but the naked rock of the hillside.

Jerry looked out toward the wide mouth of the cove. The waters of the lake were dark and deserted. A cool wind was flowing across the hills, rippling the water. It was deathly quiet.

Buck crawled out of the tiny cabin and yawned widely. Whitey came out, draped in a blanket, like a small sized Indian. "Watchman, tell us of the night," he said.

"While *we* were watching, someone was watching *us*," said Jerry quietly. He told them of seeing the cigarette smoker up on the hillside.

Buck picked up the axe. "Lead the way," he said.

Jerry jumped ashore and picked up a hefty piece of driftwood. "Hand me the field glasses, Whitey," he said. He threw the cased glasses over his shoulder and walked quietly up the wash followed closely by Buck.

Jerry climbed up the hillside, and just about where he had seen the smoker, he found a depression amid the dark rock. A half dozen cigarette butts had been thrust into the sand. Footprints and handprints showed here and there on the floor of the depression.

Buck picked up one of the cigarettes and sniffed at it. "They haven't been here very long," he said.

Jerry looked along the side of the hill. It was hopeless to think of trying to trail anyone on that bare rock. He looked down at the cove and beyond it toward Virgin Basin. The only sign of life anywhere in that vast area was the light-colored head of Whitey Cramer bobbing about in the grounded boat.

Buck rubbed his jaw. "Maybe he went back up the wash to a car," he suggested.

Jerry nodded. "Or across this point to the far side, or anywhere else they might have moored their boat for the night."

"Gives you an eerie feeling," said Buck.

Jerry uncased the field glasses and swept the surrounding terrain with them. He climbed higher and scanned the area again. Nothing. The dawn was flushed against the eastern sky, etching the distant peaks against it. It was as though the three boys had somehow been taken from earth during the night and dropped on some unknown planet, the only living things there. High over the lake a dark spot showed, like a scrap of charred paper against the gray sky. It was a hawk on an early morning reconnaissance for prey. Jerry was almost glad to see it.

They walked down to the boat and caught the pungent odor of fresh coffee on the morning wind. Whitey filled their cups as they told him of what they had seen, or *hadn't* seen, which was more exact.

"We'll take off in a few minutes," said Jerry. "It isn't likely we'll be bothered by them. This is Saturday morning. By noon these waterways will be dotted with boats. Safety in numbers."

"Yeh," said Whitey, "except that in one of those boats will be those three characters."

They stowed their gear and slid the boat into deeper water, started the engine and moved slowly out of the cove with Buck handling *Huntress*. Jerry looked up at the deserted hills, now bright with the morning sunlight on them. There was nothing to see, but he had the uncanny feeling that someone was watching them.

"Look!" said Whitey.

The sun had glinted sharply from something high on the great point that thrust itself out into Virgin Basin. Just as though it had reflected from polished glass.

Whitey snatched up the field glasses and scanned the area where they had seen the flashing. He shook his head. "Nothing but rock," he said.

Buck raised a hand and closed it into a big fist. "I'd like to catch one of them for a few minutes," he said. "I'd like to ask him a few questions."

The sun shone brightly from the metallic blue of the

lake as they moved out of the V-shaped area that opened into Virgin Basin from Detrital Wash. There were literally dozens and dozens of coves and inlets biting into the land mass to starboard, any one of which might have a clue to the fate of Charles Hunter. Jerry's heart seemed to sink within him.

"Like looking for a needle in the biggest haystack in the world," said Whitey.

Buck turned the boat toward the narrow mouth of a cove, throttling down to trolling speed. "Get up forward, Whitey," he said. "Watch for rocks."

That was only the beginning. By high noon, as they sat in the boat, eating corned beef sandwiches and drinking Cokes from the big camper icebox, they had been in at least a score of the inlets, with no results other than a long scratch on the white hull of *Huntress* and a dent in her metal cutwater from hitting some unseen obstacle beneath the water.

The humming of distant motors came to them. Virgin Basin was filling up with boats of all sizes and descriptions. A sailboat was reaching slowly across the wide basin. A plane droned high overhead. The heat was beating down into the narrow coves and inlets and a heat haze was shimmering from the naked rock high above the water level.

Whitey pulled his battered cap low over his eyes. "Which way was the wind blowing the night of the storm when your uncle disappeared, Jerry?" he asked.

Jerry racked his memory. "From due west I think."

Buck nodded. "Maybe a little more south though."

Whitey opened another Coke and took a swallow of it. "Then it's hardly likely any debris would wash up in this arm of the basin," he said. He stabbed a finger down on the lake chart. "The wind would drive debris or an overturned boat toward the northeast instead of down this way, southeast, wouldn't it?"

Buck looked at Jerry, and Jerry raised his eyebrows. "Go on, Whitey," he said.

Whitey studied the map. He traced the course of the wind that had blown that tragic night and placed a finger beyond East Point on the rugged headlands below towering Bonelli Peak. "Then anything that floated would likely end up somewhere along this stretch, well up into Overton Arm's east shore. Eh?"

"Eh!" said Buck.

Jerry looked along the land mass to their right. The heat haze danced and shimmered from the baking rock. It wasn't exactly the coolest spot-on Lake Mead that May Day. "It will take us at least another weekend to comb this area," he said.

Buck started the motor and drove the boat up the inlet toward the more open water. "Then it's the east shore of Overton?" he asked over his shoulder.

"Yep," said Whitey. He fashioned another sandwich and handed it to Buck. "This will give you the needed lift for the long crossing, mate."

Jerry studied the map. Whitey had formed a good deduction, though it was extremely nebulous. Uncle Chuck's boat could hardly sink, even though it had been made of aluminum, for the flotation tanks and the Styrofoam used inside the hull would have kept it afloat, even though awash. Why hadn't someone spotted the wreckage or at least parts of the boat if it had been torn to pieces by the elements? That was something that had bothered everyone who knew that lake and had known about *Explorer*, the boat that Uncle Chuck had been using when he had vanished.

Huntress skirted a point that protruded far out into the

arm and Buck set his course for the distant shore. A large, twin-engine outboard boat was coming slowly into Detrital Wash, the sun gleaming from its paint and metalwork, the spray flying brightly from the dipping bows. Jerry focused the glasses on it. The boat seemed too large for the one they had vaguely seen the night before, but at night one could not be a sure judge of such a thing. Nor could he possibly recognize any of the men who had been in the mysterious boat looking for *Huntress* and her crew.

The distant sailboat came about and slanted back across the wide basin. A fast catamaran outboard shot past it, both powerful engines roaring and throwing up sparkling rooster tails from the spinning propellers. A quartet of girls in bathing suits were in the wide cockpit. Buck whistled softly. "Now why couldn't it have been *them* who came after us last night?"

Whitey grunted. "If they had seen that face of yours, it would have spoiled the whole thing. Now, if they had seen *me*..."

Buck shook his head. "Girls like that like *men*, sonny, not seventeen-year-old children."

Jerry studied boat after boat. There had been nothing distinguishing about the one that had almost run into them the night before. Nothing outstanding about it. They had not been able to see the registration number. There were many boats of all sizes, shapes, and coloring, powered with all makes and horsepower of outboard motors, and many of the boats were inboards, some of them quite large. He recognized some of them from the marina.

"Hopeless," said Whitey. "They could be in any of those boats. I can see a half dozen of them, about the same size and shape as the one we saw."

Buck looked back. "One faint clue we have about them is that those cigarettes were handmade. Bull Durham."

Whitey rolled his eyes upward. "Bull Durham," he said. "My dad still smokes Bull Durham!"

"Maybe it was him sitting up there," said Buck, "watching over his little boy."

One motorboat crossed the wake of a big cruiser and came toward *Huntress*. Jerry eyed it. It was about the same size and shape as the unknown boat of the night before. It was about a twenty-footer, with a small cabin forward, and a powerful motor that drove it easily through the water. One man was at the wheel, handling the boat. Another sat in a chair in the wide cockpit, looking toward *Huntress*. Jerry reached for the glasses, but as he raised them the boat turned toward Detrital Wash and roared away, throwing up a wide sparkling wake. Jerry couldn't read the registration number, nor see any name on the hull. Neither of the men looked back at *Huntress*. In a matter of minutes, it had vanished around a rocky point.

"Waste of time," said Buck. "Me, I'm going across this basin to look for clues and I ain't going to let anyone bother me."

"He's angry," said Whitey in a kindly tone.

"And hot," said Buck. "How's for a swim when we get over there?"

Jerry nodded. "Open her up," he said. "Let's see what she can do."

Huntress responded magnificently. Jerry smiled, then saw Whitey peering over the side. "What's bothering that egghead of yours?" he asked.

Whitey rubbed his jaw. "She's cavitating a little," he said.

"Listen to him!" jeered Buck.

Whitey patted Buck on the shoulder. "Throw her into a few fast turns," he suggested.

The boat seemed to skid in the water as Buck threw her into hard right and left turns.

"Well?" said Jerry.

Whitey nodded. "Fasten a couple of stabilizers on each side of the stern, say three or four feet long, add a pad to the bottom, and this boat will make a couple more knots. I'll guarantee it."

Jerry looked at Buck. Buck shrugged. "Once in a while the little man thinks of something real bright," he said.

Whitey casually inspected his fingernails. "We keep fooling around on this lake, being followed by the Three Unknowns, and we might just have to have a mite more speed. That wasn't exactly Mixmasters they had hanging onto the transom of that boat last night. They've got power to spare, men."

As usual, Whitey could call a shot without much effort. The kid had a well-earned reputation for figuring out intricate problems. He was usually all thumbs with tools. It was Jerry who had done the tougher parts of the wood and metalwork on the boat, while Buck seemed to be more at home with his greasy hands buried in motor parts. It was Whitey who could do the headwork, and he was rarely wrong.

They had crossed the basin by now and Buck throttled down the motor, coasting easily and slowly into a high-walled cove that was still comparatively shaded from the burning sun. The anchor plunged into the water. *Huntress* swung into the wind. Minutes later three brown bodies hit the water one after the other.

Chapter 3

The Mysterious Fisherman

THE LONG HOT DAY HAD DRAGGED ITSELF toward dusk. *Huntress* swung idly at anchor in yet another cove, one of the many she had poked her sleek bows into that day. Most of the coves were empty of life, though now and again there had been boats moored in them, or grounded on the shore, while fishermen tried their luck. *Huntress* was now situated well within the high-walled cove, out of sight of anyone who might come into the cove.

Buck's head poked up out of the water, complete with face mask and snorkel. He pulled himself over the side and took off the mask and the huge flippers from his feet.

"Find anything?" said Jerry. There wasn't much hope in his voice.

"Nothing but empty beer cans and soda pop bottles," said Buck. "So many of them it's a wonder we didn't run aground on them."

"No use looking any further today," said Jerry.

Buck shook his head. He was tired. He had spent a

good part of the afternoon in the water, and a large part of that time *under* the water. "This is as hopeless as the coves on the Detrital Wash arm," he said. "Jerry, this is a mighty big lake."

"We've still got tomorrow," said Whitey as he opened a soup can and poured the contents into a saucepan.

"What's on the menu tonight?" asked Buck.

"Glurp," said Whitey.

Buck nodded in satisfaction. Whitey was famous for his "glurp," an amazing concoction of anything he happened to have on hand, never quite the same ingredients, but always tasting about the same, and consistently delicious. His deft use of herbs, spices, and other odds and ends would have done credit to a master chef.

Jerry watched Whitey ladling in more ingredients. "The Sorcerer's Apprentice," he said.

Buck crawled into his bunk. "Call me for chow," he said. He was asleep in minutes.

Jerry was refueling the gas tank from a spare can when suddenly he raised his head. Whitey looked quickly at him. Jerry raised a finger to his lips. The cove was still and quiet. The water was without a ripple, as flat as a sheet of painted tin. Something had splashed near the entrance to the cove. If it had been a fish, it was a lunker. Jerry glanced at the racked fishing rods. The fisherman was never buried very deep within any of the three friends.

Whitey turned down the flame of the gas stove. He looked toward the rock shoulder behind which *Huntress* was moored out of view of anyone in the mouth of the cove. Something splashed again.

The sun was still throwing fairly good light down into the cove, although long shadows were creeping down the hillsides above it.

The splashing sound came again. Water rippled gently and lapped against the shore. Neither of the boys moved. Then suddenly, as though manipulated by the strings of a giant puppeteer, the bow of a metal boat moved into view, followed by the gleaming aluminum hull, but as yet the boys couldn't see what power was moving it.

Whitey's eyes widened. He looked at Jerry and there was no need for him to speak. The boat had stopped, with just the forward half of it showing, and it was in the shadow of the rock shoulder. No one could be seen. There was absolutely no sound now. Jerry knew well enough what Whitey was thinking. *The mysterious boat was exactly the same size and model as* "Explorer," *the boat that had vanished along with Charles Hunter three long years before.*

Whitey's mouth opened and closed, and for once in his whole seventeen years of life he couldn't speak.

Jerry felt an icy ball form in the pit of his stomach.

The boat moved again, inch by inch, until it floated into clear view. A man sat in the stern beside an outboard motor, a paddle held in his hands, and his head moved slowly as he scanned the darkening shore. Then he turned his head to look directly at *Huntress*. He wore a wide brimmed straw hat, and the upper part of his face was shielded. A neatly trimmed mustache showed above his mouth, below a generous nose. Chuck Hunter had had such a hat, such a nose, such a mustache...

"Oh, my god," husked Whitey Cramer.

For a long and agonizing moment the figure in the boat stared at the two boys. It was absolutely quiet. Both boats were motionless on the still water.

Jerry opened his mouth but could not speak. He extended a hand, then slowly lowered it, trying to speak.

The figure moved a little. "Hi, fellas," a pleasant voice said. "How's the fishing?"

Jerry wiped the cold beads of sweat from his forehead. "We didn't do any fishing today," he said. "Just fooling around."

"Just fooling around," croaked Whitey.

The man nodded. He dipped his paddle and moved the boat closer to *Huntress*. "I thought there might be some lunkers in here," he said. "Didn't even know this cove was around here. Fools you to see that rock shoulder. First thing you know, here is the cove. Can't hardly see it from out in the basin."

"Yeh," said Jerry.

"Well, I won't poach on your fishing grounds."

"'S'all right," said Whitey weakly.

The man shook his head. "Getting dark. Got to get back to my camp over at Middle Point."

"Don't run on the lake after dark without lights," said Jerry.

"I know better than to do that." The man let the boat drift a little closer. "Nice boat you got there. Belong to your dad, son?"

"My uncle," blurted out Jerry.

"Looks familiar somehow."

"Hasn't been in the water for three years," said Whitey. He winced as a foot came down on his left instep.

"So?" The man smiled. "Your uncle just bought her, eh?"

"No," said Jerry. The man was too inquisitive to suit him.

The boat came closer, and the man sized up the two boys in the cockpit. "Maybe I'll stay in here tonight," he said.

Buck came up out of the cabin and stood there silhouetted against the sky, broad shouldered and big, actually looking bigger than he was because of the indefinite light.

"On the other hand," said the man, "maybe I better get back to the other side. Got my tent set up there."

"Yeh," said Buck.

The man let the boat drift a little. He felt in his shirt pocket and brought out a sack of makings, then deftly rolled a cigarette. He snapped a match on his thumbnail and lit the cigarette, watching the three boys through the Hare of the match. *"Adios,"* he said. He stood up and started the outboard motor, then sat down and steered it in a wide sweep away from the *Huntress.* In a moment he was gone from sight, leaving the mingled odor of tobacco and gasoline fumes drifting on the quiet air. *Huntress* bobbed and curtsied in the wash from the other boat. The water lapped softly on the shore.

Whitey relighted the stove. "Bull Durham," he said.

Jerry looked at Buck. "You hear everything?"

"Yep."

"What do you think?"

Buck shrugged. *"Quién sabe?* Who knows?"

"Looks like another big night," said Whitey. "Eat hearty, for tonight we stand guard."

The distant sound of the motor died away. The wind murmured softly through the dry brush high on the shore.

"That was about the same kind of boat your uncle had, wasn't it?" asked Buck, as he began to fill his plate.

"Something like it," admitted Jerry.

Buck placed an English muffin in the center of his plate and heaped glurp over it. "Seems like a fella could have almost mistaken it for *Explorer.* Gave me a bit of a jolt to see it floating there." He laughed. "Of course a guy would have to be *some* kind of a *nut* to think it actually was *Explorer,* and Charles Hunter. How about that?"

"How about it?" said Whitey weakly.

"Some kind of a nut," said Jerry.

Neither one of them would look at Buck, who sat down on the side of the cockpit and began eating, but his amused eyes flicked at them now and then and they knew right well what he was thinking.

Whitey emptied his plate and drained his coffee cup.

"This place is too quiet to suit me, fellas," he said. "You know me. Ol' Whitey Cramer, the fella who loves the sparkle of lights and the cheery sound of music. Maybe we ought to move somewhere else, just for tonight of course. Ha! Ha! Ha!"

"March order," said Jerry. "Shove off and all that! *Andale!*"

It was a matter of minutes to up anchor, start the motor, and head out into Virgin Basin. It was dark enough for the running lights, but no one suggested putting them on. If the patrol spotted them, it would cost them a heavy fine, and no excuse they could offer would save them from it, but the present situation was an emergency in their minds, and they'd have to risk it.

Huntress surged through the darkness with Jerry at the wheel, while his two companions peered through the thickening darkness to port and starboard watching for other boats. Far across the dark basin they saw the winking lights of other boats, but there weren't any within a half mile of *Huntress.*

Jerry took a chance, once they were well away from the shore, and opened the boat up for all she was worth. She tore along with a bone in her teeth and a wide wake spreading out frothy white on the dark waters. Then Jerry spotted the distant flashing white light on East

Point to starboard, indicating the channel that led into Virgin Canyon.

"Where to?" asked Whitey.

Jerry shrugged. "We can cross over to the starboard side of the channel and into the bay past Napoleon's Tomb and stay there tonight."

"Napoleon's *Tomb?*" asked Whitey.

"There's always the Campanile."

"How about Temple Bar Landing?" suggested Whitey.

Jerry grinned. "Nice and lively there, eh, Whitey? Nothing like Fremont Street in Vegas, but lively enough for you."

They could see lights approaching from up channel, and several other boats coming across from the far side of Virgin Basin. Jerry flicked on the running lights. Far ahead of him he could see the flashing red light that marked the point to the north of the Campanile. They had a good seven or eight mile run before they'd reach Temple Bar Landing.

"Maybe we ought to try farther up the lake tomorrow," said Buck.

"I wonder," said Jerry quietly. He looked at the face of his close friend. "My uncle used to say the darker the night out on the water, the bigger the lake got and the smaller your boat. Well, day or night, Buck, this is one whale of a big lake to look for clues on a man who vanished three years ago."

"Never say die, Jerry," said Whitey.

"There speaks the brave, undaunted heart," said Buck dryly.

They came into Temple Bar Landing and ran the boat aground. The place was dotted with the twinkling lights of campfires, trailers, and moving cars coming in on the road from US 93, twenty-eight miles away. There were many boats in the area; some moored offshore, others resting on the beach. The hum of life came to the three boys.

"Let's walk over and get a hamburger," suggested Whitey.

"After all that glurp?" protested Buck.

"He wants to see the gay night life of Temple Bar," said Jerry.

"He can go without me then. I'm beat," said Buck.

Whitey stepped over onto the shore. "Some fellas can take it and others can't," he said. "Come on, Jerry. It's on Old Dad."

They trudged along the shore, eyeing the boats. A radio was playing from a big inboard cruiser lying offshore. A girl laughed gaily.

"Look," said Whitey suddenly.

A boat had been drawn up on the shore. Once again Jerry recognized the same type and size of boat as *Explorer* had been, and the same type the stranger had paddled into the cove earlier that evening. There was no one near it. Whitey walked over and looked at it.

"Well?" asked Jerry.

Whitey nodded. "It's the same boat," he said. "See the dent on the port bow? The deep gouge along the waterline? Same motor too, Jerry."

"Yeh," said Jerry. He looked along the shore.

"On the other hand, maybe I better get back to the other side. Middle Point. Got my tent set up over there," mimicked Whitey in a perfect imitation of the stranger's voice.

"Well, maybe he changed his mind," said Jerry.

"Yeh."

They walked on for a hundred yards, then Whitey

looked at Jerry. "That sure isn't the boat those three characters were in." No.

Whitey slogged on. "Maybe they have *two* boats," he said quietly.

"You and your imagination!"

Whitey kicked an empty can up into the air and ran forward to field it neatly. He dropped it in a refuse container. "Don't be a litterbug! The litter you save may be your own, or something." He looked back at Jerry. "Maybe you have some better ideas?"

Jerry shook his head. He looked out toward the open water. The feeling that they had been watched all day had never left him, and even now, in the middle of this busy and noisy encampment, the feeling would not leave him. He was glad for once that it was a Saturday night. During the week, most of the camping areas were deserted.

On the way back to the boat, after Whitey had consumed two hamburgers and several packaged pastries, they looked for the metal boat so similar to *Explorer*. It was gone.

Far out in the dark channel two boats were moving down the lake, toward Virgin Basin. They were close together, as though traveling in company. There was nothing unusual in that, many boat parties traveled together on Lake Mead. Yet the thought came to Jerry that maybe Whitey was right. Maybe the inquisitive strangers had two boats.

"We can shove off before dawn," said Whitey as they neared *Huntress*. "Before anyone is stirring. By the time it's light we can be well on our way to wherever we decide to hunt tomorrow."

"Maybe you're tired of hunting."

Whitey looked at Jerry, then placed a hand on Jerry's

shoulder. "Sometimes you make noises like a kook," he said.

Buck was sound asleep when they entered the boat. There wasn't any reason to keep guard that night. They'd hardly be bothered by anyone in such a populous camping area. As they settled down in the cockpit, letting Buck have the entire cabin, such as it was, to himself, Whitey suddenly sat up. "Next time," he said, "I'll make dang sure no one sneaks up on us."

"You aim to set bear traps on the shore and mines in the water?" asked Jerry dryly.

"Nope! I'm going to bring Scat, my dog, along. He isn't much for looks, and he isn't too bright, but he can smell a stranger a mile away and upwind at that!"

"You can say the same thing about anyone within half a mile of Scat," said Buck sleepily from the cabin.

"I like you better when you're asleep, Buck," said Whitey sweetly.

Jerry lay back on his bed. He looked up at the dark sky, stippled with glittering stars. He had no idea where to hunt next. They had but one day left, on this trip anyway, and a good part of that day would be used up in traveling back to the marina. If they got a start before dawn, as Whitey had suggested, they'd still have at least eight hours in which to continue the hunt. The problem, as always, was *where* to hunt.

They were awake in the predawn darkness. Whitey had a natural alarm clock in his teeming brain. Temple Bar Landing slept in the cool dawn air. Not a soul was stirring, and not a light showed in building, tent, trailer, or boat.

Jerry shivered as he waded into the water shoving *Huntress* from the shore. He swung up onto her bow deck as she floated free and took a paddle. He dipped the paddle into the dark water and turned the head of the boat out toward the open water, while Whitey and Buck paddled near the stern on each side of the cockpit. The only sound was the dipping of the paddles and the lapping of the water against the sides of the boat. A current tugged at them when they were a hundred yards from the shore and drifted them out still further. Buck started the motor and flicked on the running lights. Jerry pointed upstream and *Huntress* moved steadily out into the middle of the channel. Buck turned her around the long point of land and into the center of the channel to travel up it.

When the dawn light flooded the country, they were well past the Temple, with Temple Mesa looming to port. Whitey was rattling pots and pans in the part of the cockpit he called the "galley." Jerry stood up behind the windshield with the field glasses in his hands. There was no sign of other boats on the still dark waters. A cold wind rippled the surface.

"Where to?" asked Buck.

"Head up toward Virgin Canyon. We'll take a looksee around there. We can poke in and out of coves and bays for quite a while around there," said Jerry.

After he had eaten, Jerry relieved Buck at the wheel. The sun was fully up when they passed Salt Springs Wash to starboard. The mouth of a cove loomed up to port in the entrance to Virgin Canyon. Jerry turned toward it. He looked back over his shoulder. A boat was just rounding the point far behind them. Jerry gunned the motor and drove swiftly toward the dark mouth of the cove. He looked back again but could not see the other boat. *Huntress* passed into the cove. Jerry grinned back at his two friends. "Slick as grease," he said.

"Maybe we better keep an eye out for submerged rocks," said Whitey.

"Looks deep enough," said Jerry. He gave the motor more throttles and turned sharply past a mound of rock that thrust itself up from the surface of the dark water like a warning finger. Something rang metallically. The boat shuddered and the motor sounded different. Jerry throttled back and the shuddering stopped. He moved the throttle forward and instantly the motor throbbed, and *Huntress* seemed to shiver to her very keel. Jerry stopped the motor and let the boat drift.

"Well?" said Whitey at last.

"Sounds like we nicked the prop," said Buck. He walked back to the motor and tilted it up out of the water. He looked at the propeller. "Yup," he said quietly.

"I said we ought to keep an eye out for submerged rocks," said Whitey.

"So we didn't," said Jerry shortly.

Whitey looked quickly at Jerry. "Well, it was only a suggestion," he said.

"You always have suggestions, don't you?"

Whitey flushed. "I didn't mean to criticize you, Jerry."

Jerry stood up and stepped around the windshield to drop the anchor. "Then keep your mouth shut!"

Whitey looked back at Buck. Buck held up his hands, palms upward, and shrugged. He placed a hand across his mouth in a signal for Whitey to shut up.

Jerry looked back at them. "Well," he said harshly, "you can say what you're thinking. Can we straighten out that prop, Buck?"

Buck shook his head.

"Can we use it to go back?"

"At very low speed, Jerry. No use trying to go any further today."

It was very quiet in the cove. The humming of a motor came toward the cove, roared past, then faded into the distance of Virgin Canyon.

"So we'll have a nice leisurely cruise back to the marina," said Jerry.

"Yup," said Buck. "Take us a good part of the day too."

Buck let the motor down into the water. Jerry pulled up the anchor and then started the motor, throttling as low as possible. There was some vibration, but not too serious, as long as he kept her at lowest speed. He moved her out toward the entrance. The other boys sat quietly behind him. Jerry felt like an ass. It had been his fault, but his pride wouldn't let him admit it.

Huntress bobbed a little as she met the current of the channel. Jerry turned her to travel down channel toward Virgin Basin. "I'll remember *that* place," he said grimly. "What's the name of it, Whitey?"

Whitey looked at the chart. There was a long silence.

"Well?" demanded Jerry.

"You really want to know?" asked Whitey quietly.

"Yes!"

"Little Jackass Cove," said Whitey in a very small voice.

Jerry began to laugh so hard the tears ran down his face and his stomach ached.

Buck looked at Whitey. "I guess our boy has come back to us," he said.

Chapter 4

The Question of Lost Canyon

HUNTRESS HAD BEEN SITTING IN THE HUNTER garage for almost two weeks, and in that time, stabilizers had been added to her sides forward of the transom and a plywood pad had been secured to the bottom, as Whitey Cramer had suggested. The old propeller had been traded in for a new one, of different pitch, which promised to give more speed and efficiency. Between schoolwork, part time jobs, and work on the boat, there had been no time for any other activities for the firm of Hunter, Lyon, and Cramer. Indeed, the materials and other items required for the work had put the firm in a financial hole.

"Tomorrow is Friday," said Buck Lyon as he finished removing tools and bits of wood and material from the cockpit of the boat.

Whitey Cramer crawled from beneath the trailer with a grease gun in his hand. "I can make it tomorrow afternoon if you two can."

Jerry coiled an extra nylon line and placed it in the cockpit. "I'm ready to go," he said.

"Yeh," said Buck. "But where? We didn't get a single clue the last time we were out. I'm not trying to discourage you, Jerry, but we've got to take a different tack. We could spend all year out on that lake the way we have to operate and know nothing more about your uncle than we know now."

Jerry leaned against the side of the boat. "I've been looking through Uncle Chuck's things. My folks are staying in Las Vegas with friends tonight to see some of the new shows out on the Strip. My mother said it was all right for you two characters to stay here. We've got a half day off tomorrow. We can have *Huntress* in the water by one o'clock. Okay?"

"It's fine with me," said Whitey. "I'll keep looking even if Ol' Muscles here has turned chicken on us."

"It isn't that!" protested Buck. "I want to find out what happened as much as you two do, but you've got to admit we're going about it the hard way."

"That's why I want you to stay with me tonight," said Jerry. "We can look over some of the things I dug up. There might be a clue in them somewhere."

"If we can keep Whitey away from TV," said Buck. "I think there's at least one thirty-year-old movie on tonight. Or maybe it's *The Birth of a Nation.*"

"The tube burned out," said Jerry. "Let's eat."

While they were eating, they talked about anything but their quest to find Charles Hunter. It had been about all they had conversed about since Jerry's father had agreed to let them use the boat. After all, there were other things to talk about, but when the meal was finished; it was almost a relief for Jerry to take his two partners to the small guest house at the rear of the long Hunter lot where Uncle Chuck had lived before he had vanished.

Jerry usually studied in the guest house, and it always seemed to him that the soul of Charles Hunter still occupied the place, as it was full of reminders of the man. One could form a pretty clear picture of the kind of man Charles Hunter had been by studying those rooms. Rifles were racked, and rods and reels hung on pegboard, and there were row after row of books on lost mines, treasures, legends and lore of the southwest, boating, geology, fishing and hunting, as well as histories and biographies of the West. There were maps and charts, almanacs and booklets of the southwest and the Lake Mead area in particular.

"You said something about Major Powell the last time we were out on the lake," said Whitey to Jerry.

Jerry nodded. "Powell came through in '69."

"Maybe he was looking for relics of Powell," said Buck.

Jerry shook his head. "I don't think so. He once said if Powell had left anything behind it would be long buried or swept away by now. Besides, Powell was only trying to run the Colorado for the first time. He was hardly interested in hunting for gold or anything like that."

"There are some small towns beneath the lake," said Whitey.

Jerry shook his head. "They'd have been cleaned out long before the lake flowed over their sites."

"How about the lost city up Overton Arm?" said Buck.

"Indian ruins don't have real treasure in them," said Jerry. "Artifacts and such. Uncle Chuck wasn't much interested in them beyond a sort of a curiosity about them."

Buck waved an arm. "With all these books, maps, charts, and things we surely ought to get a lead."

Whitey sat down on the sofa. "That's just it. He had so many interests it's hard to say just exactly what he was looking for."

"Yeh," said Buck. "I never thought of it that way."

Whitey looked at the fishing rods. "You were with him not long before he disappeared, Jerry," he said. "On a seven-day trip, wasn't it?"

"Yes."

"Maybe he was working around the area where he was looking for something."

"It was a fishing trip," said Buck.

Jerry narrowed his eyes. He looked at Whitey. "I never thought of it that way, Whitey. Come to think of it, we only fished for meals now and then."

"What did you do the rest of the time?" asked Whitey.

"Just poked about. I was collecting mineral specimens then, for my father. We found quite a few of them."

"Where?" asked Whitey.

Jerry walked to the large wall map of the Lake Mead area and studied it. "Man," he said quietly, "we sure poked into an awful lot of places."

"Did he act like he had found anything in there?" said Buck.

Jerry rubbed his head. The passage of three years had dulled his memory. They had had a fine time, of that he was sure, for that memory at least had not left him.

"You could pinpoint a few places," said Whitey. "Was it anywhere in the Lower Basin?"

"We just crossed into Boulder Canyon."

"Overton Arm?"

"Not that trip."

"Around the Virgin Basin?"

Jerry stared at the map on the wall, trying to fit pieces of memory back into place. "We camped one night at Detrital Wash. I don't remember looking around there very much."

"Go on."

Jerry bit his lip. "The next night, as I recall, we camped on the eastern side of the lake, around the Haystacks. We fished there the next morning, with no luck, then went on to Salt Springs Wash. We had had some trouble with the motor, so Uncle Chuck worked on it there. It was late afternoon when we went on, toward Virgin Canyon, camping that night at Hualapai Wash."

"And all that time you just fooled around, no serious searching or anything like that?" questioned Buck.

Jerry nodded.

"The next day?" asked Whitey.

Jerry scratched his head with both hands. "We went up to Iceberg Canyon, passed through it, and camped somewhere beyond Rattlesnake Cove. The next morning we crossed the channel toward the east shore. We spent the next three days along that stretch of the river."

"Maybe that's where we should be hunting then," said Buck.

Jerry turned. "The last time he was seen it was on Virgin Basin, a long way from where we spent most of those seven days."

"Heading east," said Whitey thoughtfully. "That was the day *before* the storm, wasn't it?"

"Yes."

Whitey stood up and looked at the map. "Maybe he wasn't caught by the storm. He had had plenty of time to get miles beyond Virgin Basin, and there's hardly any real wide areas of water beyond Virgin Basin. A boatman like Chuck Hunter, with a good boat like *Explorer,* would hardly get into trouble on narrow waters no matter how much the wind blew."

"I never believed he had drowned," said Buck Lyon firmly.

Jerry looked at the map. "Maybe we have been looking in the wrong places."

Whitey traced a finger along the course of the river beyond Iceberg Canyon. "Somewhere along here then," he suggested. He looked back at Jerry. "You'd better sharpen your memory, man, because me and Uncle Buck are going to take you into every cove, indentation, and empty pop bottle along there until you remember exactly where it was the two of you spent all that time."

In the silence that followed a fly buzzed lazily through the room. A moth fluttered softly against a screen.

"Lost Canyon!" said Jerry suddenly.

They stared at him.

"Lost Canyon!" Jerry plucked a worn and tattered map from a shelf and spread it out on the table. He traced the course of the Colorado on it, in the days when it had raged unchecked to the Gulf of California. It took him a moment or two to figure out where he had been with his uncle three years ago. "Somewhere around here," he said, touching a finger on a place where the Colorado coursed northerly before turning sharply to the west, then sharply south to run unchecked into Virgin Canyon.

Whitey eyed the old map. "Don't see any Lost Canyon marked on that," he said.

Buck was studying the modern wall map. "Ain't any on here neither," he said inelegantly.

"I didn't expect to find it marked on either map," said

Jerry quietly, "but I remembered Uncle Chuck talking about a lost canyon in that area."

"You mean Lost Canyon, or a *lost* canyon?" asked Whitey.

"What difference does it make?" demanded Buck.

Whitey looked at his big friend with a kindly eye. "Just this, Muscles: If it is just a lost canyon, it might have another name or no name at all. If it is Lost Canyon, and Chuck Hunter called it that, then someone else ought to know something about it."

"Yeh, small man, but *who?*"

"Somebody, that's all!"

"Big help!"

Jerry rubbed his jaw and eyed both maps. Whitey was making sense, as usual. No matter how much Jerry flogged his memory, the association of the name Lost Canyon would bring up nothing else from the dim mental files.

"Go get some Cokes, Whitey," said Buck.

Whitey left the guest house, and they could hear him whistling softly as he walked toward the Hunter house.

"Little sonofagun," said Buck. "He makes a guy like me feel like I'm all meat and no brains."

Jerry nodded. "Each to his own," he said. "Sometimes he wears me a little thin, but I have to admit he makes a man use what brains he has."

"You doing any better?" asked Buck.

Jerry shook his head. "The best I can offer is that we go back to where Uncle Chuck and I spent the last days of our trip in there. Maybe something will come up."

"Like those characters that were following us."

Jerry looked quickly at his friend. "Haven't seen hide nor hair of them since we sneaked away from them."

"That doesn't mean they're not still around."

"Well, since I haven't seen them, I'm not going to worry about them."

They heard Whitey's feet grating on the gravel pathway. The door opened and Whitey appeared.

"Where's the Cokes!" said Buck.

Whitey touched a finger to his lips. He closed the door behind him. "Listen," he said tensely. "I went into the kitchen to get the Cokes. The house was dark. When I opened the refrigerator door, it cast a light on the nearest window. I heard someone make a noise, then run along the side of the house. I shut the refrigerator door and ran through to the front of the house in time to see a man jump into the rear of a car. There was someone else driving. The wheels sure kicked up gravel, I tell you."

Buck walked to the door and reached for the knob. "Just someone who saw the house dark maybe figured no one was around. There have been a few houses burglarized around here the past few months."

"Yeh," said Whitey quietly. "But I saw the face of the man at the wheel. The streetlight was shining on him."

"So?" said Buck.

Whitey swallowed. "The last time I saw him he was sitting in a boat right near *Huntress*. Big nose, mustache and all."

"You're kidding," said Buck.

Whitey shook his head. "I saw him, Buck. You can take my word for it."

Buck looked at Jerry. "You weren't going to worry about them," he said quietly.

"They're not going to stop me from looking for my uncle," said Jerry quickly. "I don't care who or what they are."

"I sure wish we knew what your uncle had been hunting for," said Whitey.

"There's one way to find out," said Jerry. "Go back to where he and I spent those last days on that trip we made."

"Amen," said Buck.

Jerry opened the door. "I'll get the grub," he said. "Buck, you take a looksee up and down the street. Whitey, you stay here on guard."

"Guarding what?" asked Whitey.

"I don't know, but they didn't follow us two weeks ago because they wanted to burglarize my house. They're interested in what Uncle Chuck was looking for. With all these papers and maps in here, we might be sitting right on top of the solution. I'll lock up the house. We'll bunk out here tonight."

Buck met Jerry as he came from the house carrying enough supplies to nourish Whitey through the long night. "Nothing," he said.

They locked the guest house door behind them and Jerry placed the food in the little refrigerator. He took a shotgun from the gun rack and loaded it, leaning it near the door. He loaded an automatic pistol and placed it on the table. "Don't pick your teeth with that, sonny," he said to Whitey.

"You wouldn't shoot at anyone who might try to get in here, would you?"

"Try me," said Jerry quietly. "Just try me..."

Buck grinned. "Maybe we ought to rig some trip wires or something like that."

"I can go home and get Scat," suggested Whitey.

Buck shook his head. "I won't sleep in the same house with that mutt."

"Yeh," said Whitey. "I just remembered he feels the same way about you."

"Grub up," said Jerry, jerking a thumb toward the

refrigerator. "From now on, there will be complete silence as we start searching through these books, maps, and other odds and ends until we can get a clue about Lost Canyon. We can't miss a thing, men."

From then on, until bedtime, the three boys searched through the mass of material left by Chuck Hunter, with no results. Jerry lay awake a long time staring up at the dim ceiling. The last thing he did before he drifted off to sleep was to offer a silent prayer that somehow, some-where, a clue would be revealed that would lead the way to solve the mystery of the disappearance of Chuck Hunter.

Twice during the night, the neighbor's big Alsatian barked savagely, and the second time, Jerry could have sworn that he had heard voices and the distant sound of a car being driven away from the end of the street, but there was no disturbance around the guest house.

Classes dragged on the next morning. Buck drove Jerry home first, then Whitey, before he went home to get his gear. Jerry's mother had invited the three of them to have lunch at the Hunter place. Marion Hunter's lunches were famous, even to Whitey Cramer, who was a well-known connoisseur of such matters.

Marion Hunter topped off the lunch with one of her own creations, a sundae that was almost too beautiful to eat. She sat down at the table and watched the three boys. "How long will you be gone this time?" she asked Jerry.

"Until Sunday."

"If the food holds out," said Whitey.

"We've got enough for a platoon," said Buck.

"That's just about enough for him then," added Jerry.

Marion Hunter smiled. "Now, boys, let Whitey alone. He just appreciates good food."

Whitey smiled. "You have an understanding heart, Mrs. Hunter." His spoon scraped the bottom of his dish. Marion Hunter got up and replaced the empty dish with a full one, as a matter of course. Whitey flourished his spoon, plucked off the maraschino cherry at the top, popped it into his mouth, and closed his eyes in deep appreciation.

"There was a phone call for you this morning," said Jerry's mother. She looked at her son.

"Yes?"

"Some man asking if *Huntress* were for sale. I told him you weren't interested."

"Right," said Jerry.

"He was quite insistent," she said. "He asked if you intended to use it this weekend and I told him that you three boys planned to go up the lake for exploring and fishing."

"Why did he ask that, Mrs. Hunter?" said Buck.

"He said he wanted to watch *Huntress* perform. He had heard you had made some improvements in her hull. He was so insistent I told him you'd be down at the marina about one o'clock, and he could see it in the water there."

Whitey's spoon stopped halfway to his mouth. He looked quickly at Jerry.

Marion Hunter began to clear the table. "Strangely enough, I thought I recognized his voice. A week ago today a man came by the house and asked if the guest house was for rent. I told him that you used it for a study, Jerry. He said he had been looking all over Boulder City for such a place to rent. He asked if he could see it. I told him that inasmuch as I didn't intend to rent it, it was hardly worthwhile for him to look at it."

Buck slanted his eyes toward Jerry, then wiped his mouth with his napkin.

Mrs. Hunter placed the dishes in the dishwasher. "Of course, I may be only imagining things. It's difficult to compare a voice to another when you hear it over the phone."

"Of course," said Whitey.

"Still…" she said thoughtfully.

"Maybe he saw *Huntress* when he was here and thought he'd like to buy it," suggested Whitey.

She shook her head. "He walked right past her last week and hardly looked at her. Said he was a traveling man who'd be working in this area for some time. Besides, you had tools and things all over the place, and grease on her white hull, so she didn't look like the lovely thing she really is."

"He also knew we wouldn't be using her last weekend if she was up on blocks," blurted out Whitey.

She turned. "What a strange thing to say, *Milburn*."

Buck grinned. *"Milburn,"* he said. "Such a lovely name."

Jerry stood up. "Have to get moving," he said quickly. "Back the pickup into the driveway, Buck. Whitey, you fill the water jugs. Thanks, Mom, for the lunch. We'll bring back some fine bass for dinner Sunday."

She looked at him thoughtfully. "You know, Gerald, I sometimes get the oddest impression that you boys are holding something back from me."

Buck had vanished. Whitey was filling the first of the water jugs. Jerry kissed his mother. "Why should I hold anything back from you?" he said.

She patted his face. "I'm sure I don't know."

The phone rang. Jerry picked it up. It was his aunt, wanting to speak with his mother. He handed the phone to his mother. "It's Aunt Alice," he said. He glanced at Whitey and jerked his head toward the door. Whitey was filling the last of the jugs. He handed one of them to Jerry and took the other two. The two of them hurried out to the boat and placed the jugs inside, lifted the trailer tongue to the hitch on the back of the truck, thrust in the electrical connection, fastened the safety chain, and walked beside the boat as Buck drove out into the street.

Whitey looked back at the house. "You think she suspects?" he asked in a dramatic voice.

Jerry shrugged. *"Quién sabe?* All I want to do is get out of here before you make another verbal slip, *Milburn."*

They stopped at Whitey's house and picked up Scat, half beagle and half spaniel, short of hock and long of hair, with a magnificent, plumed tail all out of kilter with the rest of his body, and the most soulful eyes a dog ever had. He *did* smell, but he was a good watchdog. Whitey looked at Buck as he started to get into the cab of the truck. One look was enough. He carried the dog to the rear of the truck and placed him in the back. He barely had time to regain his own seat in the cab before Buck rattled the truck off toward the Lake Mead road.

Chapter 5

Up the Colorado

THE BURNING SUN WAS SLANTING LOWER IN the west when *Huntress* surged into Boulder Canyon with Whitey Cramer at the helm. Buck sat in a folding chair in the cockpit with his eyes glued to the field glasses, watching the few boats dotting the surface of that part of the Lower Basin which was still in view. There had been a few boatmen puttering around the marina that hot Friday afternoon, but none of them seemed much interested in *Huntress* and her crew, nor had any of the boats in the Lower Basin veered toward *Huntress* as she cruised toward the upper end of the basin. It was a bit perplexing, but all of the boys felt a surge of relief within them when at last *Huntress* sped into Boulder Canyon.

Whitey expertly threaded the boat through the channel and at last they saw the wide expanse of Virgin Basin rippling under the dry wind that swept down from Overton Arm. A sailboat was moving slowly toward Overton Arm. A big cruiser had been anchored in the mouth of Boulder Wash, with swimmers splashing about it.

Whitey looked back at Jerry. "She handles different-ly," he said, "but I'd like to open her up a bit to see how that pad and those stabilizers affect her."

"Damn the torpedoes! Full speed ahead!" cried Jerry.

Whitey pushed forward the mono control and the big motor began to roar. *Huntress* lifted a little as though clearing her skirts from the water and sped across the basin like a living thing. The wake spread white across the sparkling blue water. Spray flicked up and caught the rays of the sun, turning it into an iridescent shower.

Buck looked at Jerry. "The little man was right at that," he said in a low voice, "but don't tell him I said so."

"Do I look *that* loco?"

Whitey threw the eighteen-footer from side to side. He looked back with a grin on his freckled face. "Sure stopped that cavitating," he crowed. "Notice it?"

They shook their heads.

"Notice how that pad lifts her up a little higher at the stern?"

Again, the heads waggled.

Whitey tried once more. "You see how those stabilizers keep her from squatting down in the hard turns?"

Two heads wagged as one.

Scat stuck his long brown nose out of the cabin. "Whurf!" he said.

Whitey nodded. "At least you can see the results, Scat," he said, "but then *you've* got *intelligence*."

Huntress fled across Virgin Basin and rounded East Point, where Whitey slowed her down to a steady cruising speed. She moved past Napoleon's Tomb to star-board and Hobo Point to port. They passed Sugarloaf to port with Temple Bar Landing far to starboard. It was getting dusky when Whitey turned her in toward

Hualapai Wash. There were no other boats to be seen in the deep cove that formed the anchorage. They anchored *Huntress* offshore, splashed into the water for a swim, then prepared the evening meal.

While they ate, they talked over their plans. "We'll keep anchored," said Jerry. "That way we can leave here in a hurry if anything turns up. Scat can keep watch. He's good for that at least."

Whitey fed Scat a slice of salami. "Ignore him. Scat," he said tenderly.

"How come he's called Scat?" asked Buck.

Whitey grinned. "When he was a pup, he was always getting under Mom's feet and she'd keep yelling at him. Scat! Like that."

"Whurf!" said Scat.

"That's what you yell at a cat, not a dog," said Jerry.

"That dummy doesn't know the difference," said Buck.

Whitey eyed Buck. He shook his head. "One of these dark nights," he said, "you'll be glad Scat is here to protect you."

"We'll up anchor at dawn," said Jerry.

"Aye, aye, Commodore," said Buck. "Shall we run out the guns after we double shot them, and sand the decks?"

"England expects every man to do his duty," said Whitey solemnly. He closed one eye and thrust a hand inside his shirt.

The darkness seemed to plunge into the canyons. Buck and Whitey set up the chessboard in the little cabin and started a game. Scat lay in the cockpit with Jerry, looking mournfully at the chess players. High overhead, above the darkness of the canyons, the first faint stars could be seen. The wind shifted and flowed down the canyons, bringing with it the astringent odor of dry brush and scrub trees. A fish broke water near the boat.

Jerry half closed his eyes. Time and time again he had tried to reconstruct the last few days of his trip with Uncle Chuck three years before. The number of canyons, hills, mesas, coves, and arroyos they had probed into, around or over, was a jumble in his mind. A jumble of fantastically colored rock, thorny vegetation, and thick, enervating heat. Lost Canyon. The name meant nothing. The maps and charts did not show it. It was not mentioned in any of the books left behind by Chuck Hunter. Then the thought came quickly to Jerry through the darkness of the canyons. Maybe Uncle Chuck had taken the very maps or charts that marked the site of Lost Canyon along with him on his last trip!

Jerry opened his eyes wide. He felt a cold chill of fear, almost as though the voice of Chuck Hunter had come soundlessly to him, trying to give him a hint or clue as to what had happened. He shook his head. Everything was lost in the maze of water and canyons northeast of where *Huntress* swung idly at anchor. Every tiling. The map, boat, and man. *Everything!*

"Check," said Whitey. "

Jerry looked at him, almost as though Whitey had spoken with the voice of fate. It was check, sure enough, but not checkmate and it wouldn't be checkmate, as far as Jerry was concerned, until he had positive proof of the fate of Uncle Chuck.

They moved out quietly before dawn, passing View Point and entering the long, broad reach of Gregg Basin. They were completely mobile now, for Whitey made with the pots and pans, brewing coffee, scrambling eggs and bacon, performing great feats of legerdemain, under the appreciative, though inexpressibly mournful eyes of Scat.

By the time they neared Sandy Point, the flashing white light that indicated channel course and direction out on the point had automatically flicked off for the day. The sun was flooding down into Gregg Basin when they entered Iceberg Canyon, and when they had forged through it, the heat of the day was already settling about them. They had almost a full day ahead of them, but the task that confronted them could hardly be accomplished that afternoon and the following Sunday morning.

Buck was handling *Huntress* as they cleared Iceberg Canyon and passed Boundary Point. He looked back at Jerry. "Well, at least we haven't seen any sign of our boys."

Jerry nodded. "Kind of puzzling though. They seemed so interested the last time we were on the lake, and that character who wanted to rent the guest house, and who later called the house, was certainly interested in what we were doing."

"He might have been around when we left the marina," said Buck.

"Yes." Jerry looked back into the canyon. "Haven't seen anyone following us. Beats the heck out of me."

"Where to?"

"We can start up toward Grand Wash. I can bet you we won't run into anyone up *that* way."

Huntress moved slowly up the channel of Grand Wash. They had crossed over into the state of Arizona somewhere back in Iceberg Canyon, the Nevada line reaching the channel in Driftwood Cove, coming from the north, although the southern part of the lake and the channels were in Arizona all the way back to Boulder Dam. To the east, across the towering Shivwits and Sanup Plateaus, was Grand Canyon, formed by the Colorado eons past. The channel south of Grand Wash turned east and doubled back north again beyond Lower Granite Gorge to the eastern end of the Grand Canyon. It was all wild and rugged country, hardly peopled except where the few roads cut through, and on the tourist trails in the Grand Canyon area. There were a few isolated ranches scattered about, hidden in the deep valleys.

There wasn't a soul in Grand Wash. A hawk hung in the quiet air, almost as though he were a stuffed specimen hanging in a natural history museum. Cloud puffs had started to drift across the sky, chasing their shadows up and down hill in a race that could never be won or lost. There was a dreaminess in the scene, an enveloping sense of peace and quiet. To Jerry Hunter, though, there was almost a foreboding atmosphere in the huge wash. The feeling came to him that perhaps they were closing in on the mystery of Charles Hunter's disappearance, and, in a sense, Jerry wasn't too sure he wanted one answer to the mystery the proof that his uncle was indeed dead.

Buck looked back at Jerry for directions. Jerry picked a small cove on the eastern shore, almost at random, but then they had to start somewhere. Buck cut the motor and let the momentum of the boat carry it forward to ground gently on a sandbank. There was no sound but the lapping of the tiny waves from the boat's wash against the shore and the boat, and then that too died away.

None of the boys spoke. Even Scat seemed a little awed by the seeming loneliness of the place. It was too early on Saturday for boaters to come up from the Lower Basin and, even so, Grand Wash was never crowded with boaters.

Jerry stepped over the side and walked up the shore. He eyed the terrain, but there was nothing to remind him that he had ever been there before. He walked up a shallow canyon, feeling the heat rising about him. By late afternoon the place would be almost unbearable. There was nothing up the canyon but a pile of rusted tin cans and a weather-beaten rubber shoe.

For two hours the boys probed into the nooks and crannies of the area and gained nothing but burning feet and a prodigious thirst. Scat was the smart one, as Whitey always insisted he was, for he lay comfortably in the boat, under the shade of the navy top, getting the benefit of what little coolness arose from the water.

By midafternoon the boys had been driven back to the boat. Whitey moved it slowly back toward the mouth of the wash, while Jerry studied the eastern shore as he had done earlier. Buck scanned the shore as well, using the field glasses. They had seen no other boats that day. The area seemed completely deserted.

The sun lanced its rays from the water, striking upward against the taut faces of the boys. Jerry shook his head. No chord of memory had been touched in his mind. He looked at Whitey. "Keep moving south," he said. "We'll pass through that narrow neck of the channel down toward God's Pocket. There are a lot of holes in the wall down that way."

"You feeling anything yet?" asked Whitey.

"No," admitted Jerry. Once again, the feeling had come over him that he was on a fruitless search, and that he was exposing his two good friends to the futile effort as well.

The sun was slanting westerly when at last Buck looked at Jerry. "How's for a swim?" he said.

"Where?"

Buck jerked a thumb toward the shore, picking at

random a deep indentation. "Looks like a little shade in there, Commodore."

Jerry nodded. *Huntress* moved slowly into the cove. Buck dropped the anchor and almost beat it to the bottom as he dived over the side. Bubbles swirled up through the water.

Whitey yawned. "I'll bypass the swim," he said. "How about a cold Coke?"

"Later," said Jerry. He dived over the side and struck out for the shore. He walked from the water and looked up the canyon, already thick in afternoon shadows. It seemed to end not too far from the mouth, but he had the impression that it went still further into the massive country between the Shivwits and Sanup Plateaus. The canyon did not come into his memory of that country. There were quite a few places Jerry and his uncle had not penetrated. Indeed, there were quite a few no humans had penetrated, to be recorded in written history, as far as Jerry knew.

He could hear Buck splashing about in the water and Whitey laughing. Scat barked. The echoes drifted up the quiet canyon with an eerie quality about them. Like all explorers, it was difficult for Jerry to turn back, tired and despondent as he was. What had he expected? A signpost, neatly lettered with directions, pointing toward the place of mystery?

He sat down on a rock to pick a shard of detritus from his foot. He raised his head, almost as though he felt an unseen presence somewhere near him. He looked quickly to his left, down toward the distant cove. The dying sun glinted from the bright work of the *Huntress*. An uneasiness came over him. He looked quickly to the right further into the shadowed depths of the canyon and he could have sworn he saw a furtive movement. He stared toward it but did not see anything. Jerry stood up and walked a little closer. The wind was creeping down the canyon as the day died. The scant brush moved gently. Jerry reached the place where he thought something had moved. It was as quiet and deserted as the rest of the canyon. Imagination, or perhaps the movement of some animal. Perhaps the wind.

He walked slowly down toward the cove, but the uneasy feeling persisted within him. Several times he had the feeling he was being watched. He looked back three or four times but saw nothing. He was tired and hot. The water would feel good and already he had caught the scent of cooking. Trust Whitey Cramer to have an early meal.

The feeling came to him again. He whirled. He saw nothing. As he turned to walk again toward the mouth of the canyon, he saw something on a rock face twenty feet from him carved letters, hardly legible at that distance. He walked closer to them, and a strange, almost mystical feeling came over him. "Jerry Hunter, Boulder City, May 1960," he read aloud. He had no recollection of having ever carved such letters in that canyon or any other canyon around there, for that matter.

Jerry looked back up the canyon. This time he was sure he saw a movement, but nothing could drive him to go back up there in the shadowed darkness, at least not the way he was feeling right at that moment. It was too eerie, too uncanny.

He walked down the shore and waded into the water, striking out for the boat, half hearing the battle of badinage between his two friends. He pulled himself over the side of the boat and accepted a towel from Buck.

"What's with you?" asked Whitey curiously. "Look like you saw a ghost."

Jerry told them of finding the carving on the rock wall, but not of the furtive movements he had seen, or *thought* he had seen.

Whitey began to fill the plates with one of his specialties. He looked up the dark canyon. "Maybe this is the one," he said. "Lost Canyon?"

Jerry shook his head. "I hardly think so."

"And you say you can't remember carving those letters in there?" said Buck.

"Yes."

Whitey sat down and placed his plate on his bony knees. "It's the best clue we've found yet."

"The *only* one," said Buck.

"It doesn't mean anything," said Jerry. "These canyons are full of carvings from prehistoric times up until the present."

"Wonder where it goes?" said Whitey.

"Stop wondering," said Buck. "We'll find out."

"Tonight?"

Buck grinned at Whitey. "By the light of the moon, my boy!"

"There won't be any moon tonight, or at least not much of a moon. Not enough to see anything in there anyway."

"You scared, Whitey?"

It was getting darker in the cove. Jerry lit a gas lantern. The darkness seemed to settle comfortably around the boat. "We've got a good part of tomorrow to hunt about up there," he said.

"You don't sound very interested," said Buck.

"Maybe I'm losing hope. Buck. I'm not going to let that carving build me up too much."

Buck glanced at Whitey. Whitey shook his head. "Pie

à la mode for dessert," he said cheerfully. He patted his dog on the head. "You too, Scat."

They moved the boat deeper into the cove, mooring it to a rock ledge that loomed over the water. The night was quiet. They had not heard or seen another boat all day long. This time they had eluded the mysterious men who seemed so interested in their quest to find the missing Charles Hunter.

It had been a hot and tiring day, so the boys wasted little time in getting to bed. There was no need to keep guard, for little Scat, despite two helpings of peach pie à la mode, would stand guard for them.

Jerry slept in the cockpit, letting Whitey have the other hunk in the little cabin. Whitey was a better fit in there than Jerry was, at least with Buck filling up two-thirds of the space.

Jerry's last thought, as he fell asleep, was of those movements he had seen farther up the canyon. It must have been an animal, or his imagination. *What else could it have been?*

Chapter 6

Wreckage in the Cove

JERRY AWOKE SHIVERING. HE PULLED THE blanket up about his shoulders, but it didn't do much good. He opened his eyes to see the first pale flush of the coming dawn in the sky. It was cold in the deep canyons. A chill wind whispered through the cove. Jerry reached for a sweatshirt and pulled it over his head, but by this time he was wide awake. He stood up and draped the blanket about his shoulders. The contrast with the heat of the day before was hardly believable. The movement of the boat as he walked about awoke the other two.

"Lordy!" said Whitey. "What happened? We traveling under the ice up at the North Pole?"

Jerry climbed out of the boat and stood on the rock ledge. "Let's start a fire on the shore," he said. "We can cook breakfast over it after we warm ourselves."

Buck pulled his blanket higher over his head. "Let me know when you get it started," he said.

Whitey climbed out of the boat. He and Jerry foraged for driftwood and in a short time had a warm fire blazing against a towering rock wall. The flames leaped and postured in a macabre dance all their own against the rock face. Whitey and Jerry stood there with blankets about their shoulders warming their hands by the fire.

"I'll get the gear for chow," said Whitey. He walked back to the boat and gathered what he needed to make breakfast. He also woke Buck and chased him up the beach to get firewood. Jerry helped Whitey prepare the food. After a time he looked up the canyon. There was no sign of Buck on the beach.

Whitey shook his head. "Fire getting low," he said. "That big clown should have been back by now."

Minutes ticked past and still no sign of Buck. Jerry looked up the canyon, then along the beach. Buck certainly should have been back by now. "I'll go take a looksee," he said. He started walking up the canyon, then saw something moving at the far side of the canyon mouth, not far from the water's edge. There was no mistaking Buck's broad shoulders. He walked toward Buck.

Buck turned as he heard Jerry walking toward him. "Look at tins," he said quietly. He held up a piece of weathered board.

Jerry took it from his hands. It was obviously the seat of a boat, for there were angled metal pieces at each end to fasten it to the sides of a boat. "So, Buck?" he said.

"Turn it over."

Jerry turned it over. There was a brass plate still affixed to the wood, with the name of the manufacturing company, its location, and a serial number. "Fair-weather," said Jerry.

"Wasn't Explorer a fair-weather boat?" said Buck.

"Yes." Jerry eyed the serial number. "1003," he said.

"Well?"

Jerry shook his head. "I never knew the serial number

of Explorer," he said. "Fair-weather made a lot of boats. Still does for that matter. How can we know that this was actually from Explorer unless we check back home? Even then, there might be no record of it." Jerry stepped back. Something crunched beneath his left foot and something else struck his ankle a stinging blow. For a frightening instant he thought he had been bitten by a rattler until he looked down and saw a broken boat paddle lying on the ground. There was something about that paddle that riveted his attention. Just above the blade someone had tied an intricate knot to keep the water from running along the loom of the paddle to wet the paddler's hands. The knot was a turk's head. He knew it well enough, for Chuck Hunter had taught him how to tie it. There were a number of them aboard Huntress, as drip guards on her paddles, while another marked the king spoke of the Steering wheel.

"What's the matter, Jerry?" asked Buck.

"The paddle! Uncle Chuck always worked turk's head knots on them as drip guards."

Buck whistled softly. "Yeh," he said. "You think...?"

Jerry picked up the broken paddle. He couldn't recognize it, of course, for there isn't much difference between paddles, and this one was well weathered, warped, and broken. He looked at the tangled pile of driftwood lying wedged in among the rocks. Without a word he and Buck pitched into it.

They could hear Whitey calling out to them and a little while later he appeared calling them unpleasant names for not coming back with the wood. Jerry quickly showed him their discoveries, and in a moment, Whitey was burrowing into the pile too. The odor of burning bacon and eggs drifted about the canyon, the smoke rising to meet the first rays of the morning sun.

It was Buck who pulled a battered flotation tank from under a log. There was no way of telling if it had come from *Explorer* or not, but they put it aside to check it later. There was one chilling thought each of them had, and each of them kept it to himself. If the pieces of boat had come from *Explorer,* it had been one whale of a storm that had struck the little craft. With such insensate destruction of the boat, it was hardly possible that Chuck Hunter could have survived.

There were no more relics, so they carried what they had found back to the fire and, while Whitey prepared a second breakfast, Jerry and Buck examined the wreckage. Jerry studied the tank. It was about the size of the airtight tanks that boat manufacturers fasten beneath seats to afford flotation to a boat if it is swamped. Something he saw on both sides of the tank puzzled him. "Look," he said to his two companions. He fingered the narrow holes, one on each side of the tank, then he picked up the small camp axe and neatly fitted the blade of it into each of the holes. "No rock ever punched neat holes like that," he added. "They are exactly alike and look as though they were punched through the metal with an axe something like this one."

"I don't get it," said Buck. "Why would anyone do that unless he purposefully wanted to sink a boat?"

"You're getting the idea," said Whitey quietly.

It was deathly quiet in the canyon except for the snapping of the dying fire.

"Why would Chuck Hunter do that?" said Buck at last. "Figuring of course that this tank comes from *Explorer.*"

"Chuck Hunter never did that," said Whitey.

"Then who did?" asked Buck.

There was no answer. The air of mystery had thickened again about Chuck Hunter.

Whitey stood up and kicked sand over the fire. "Let's get this gear back to the boat," he said.

Buck hefted the flotation tank. He looked out across the dark, quiet waters of the cove. "*Explorer* was aluminum," he said. "If she had been swamped, she might have kept afloat long enough to drift ashore somewhere, but she vanished as completely as Chuck Hunter did. If she was sunk on purpose she can't be very far from here, can she?"

"You're doing the talking," said Whitey. "There's a current that sets into tin's cove from out on the river. I noticed it when we came in here. Anything that gets caught in that big eddy out there might just drift in here like all that stuff up the shore where you found those pieces."

Jerry looked at the surface of the water. "Maybe there's something under there that might tell us the story," he said. "We've got about six or seven hours to do some skin diving. Let's go!"

As they carried the gear to the boat, Scat fell behind. He turned and looked up the still dark canyon and then he began to bark sharply and insistently. The boys turned. The little mongrel's tail stood out straight behind him and his lips were drawn back from his white teeth.

"What's bothering him?" said Buck.

The barking echoes fled up the canyon and died away.

The three boys looked up toward the uninviting pathway into the broken, jumbled wilderness below the Shivwits Plateau. There wasn't a sign of life. Everything was quiet and nothing moved in the windless air. Scat stood stock still looking up the canyon. He drew back his lips to reveal his teeth, then growled low in his throat. Whatever his other faults, Scat had verified Whitey's belief in him that he was a good watchdog.

"Coyote maybe?" said Buck at last.

"Maybe," said Jerry. "I might as well tell you the facts. Yesterday afternoon when I went up there, I could have sworn something moved farther up the canyon. I walked up there but there was nothing to see. Later on, after I had found my name carved on the rock face, I looked up the canyon again and was quite certain I saw a movement up there."

Buck stepped into the boat. "Two of us better dive together for safety, the third man to stay here on watch with Scat." He looked at Jerry. "You want to team up with me first?"

Jerry nodded. Buck was the best of them in underwater work. It was his ambition to join the Navy when he graduated from high school to try out for the famed underwater demolition teams used by the Navy.

They donned flippers, face masks, and snorkels, then dropped a weighted shot line over the side. It was still cold in the canyon, but the water was comparatively warm. They had sounded the bottom around the boat and found it to average fifteen to twenty feet in depth, shoaling rather rapidly toward the shore.

They stayed close together under the water. The visibility was poor as yet, for the sun had not struck the surface of the water. Jerry passed his hands over rocks, a submerged log, and several cans. Once he thought he had found another paddle, but it was only a piece of lumber worn by time and friction into the rude semblance of a paddle.

Time and time again they surfaced. The sun was

reaching into the canyon by this time and the air was warming.

"Anything doing?" asked Jerry of Whitey.

"Not a thing." Whitey grinned. "Gets kinda lonesome up here when you characters are below. I know you're down there, but the feeling you get in this place when you don't see a buddy gets on your nerves. The place is eerie enough even when you two are up here."

Buck looked down at the water. "Sure wish we had some scuba gear," he said. "Man, we'd cover the bottom of this cove in an hour."

"Well do all right," said Jerry. He dived and swam toward the murky bottom. With scuba gear, self-contained underwater breathing apparatus, they could stay under water for a considerable length of time. No use crying about it though.

Buck brushed past him, working his way along the uneven bottom. He looked like some kind of weird denizen of the deep. He glanced back at Jerry through his face mask and beckoned him on.

It was ten o'clock when at last they took the time for a rest, and hot chocolate brewed by Whitey. He reported he hadn't seen anything, or heard anything for that matter, and Scat, who was sunning himself on the forward deck, had been very quiet.

Jerry looked at his watch. "We haven't much time left," he said.

"Maybe we could stay overnight and skip school tomorrow," said Buck.

"And lose the right to use the boat?" said Jerry. "We can't do that."

"But if your father knew what we had found, Jerry?"

Jerry shook his head. "We're supposed to be bass fishing, man."

"But if he knew we had a lead on your uncle?"

"We haven't *got* a lead, Buck. Nothing but my name carved on a rock, and a few pieces of a boat, something like the one Uncle Chuck disappeared with."

"Well, supposing we do find the boat?"

"Then he'll probably turn over the matter to the authorities, and you know where they will put us."

"Yup."

Whitey began to get his skin-diving gear together. He lowered himself over the side of the boat. "I'll go down alone," he said.

Buck shook his head. "No! Two together! That's the rule!"

Whitey looked at Jerry. "How about that, Commodore? You make the decision."

"Buck is in charge of underwater operations," said Jerry.

"You greased out of that one, didn't you?"

"Take Scat," said Jerry. "He can swim better than you can anyway."

"Scat has to stand guard in case one of you lunkheads goes to sleep on the job."

"Listen!" said Buck quickly.

They could hear the steady droning of an outboard motor somewhere out in the channel. *Huntress* was hidden behind a projecting point, so she couldn't be seen from the channel. The motor droned louder and louder, almost filling the canyon with its noise, then faded away down the channel.

"Let's go," said Buck. He slid over the side and dived with Whitey.

Jerry poured another cup of chocolate. He was beginning to lose heart. They didn't have much time left to return to the marina.

It was after eleven o'clock when at last Buck and Whitey gave up. They stripped off their skin-diving gear. Neither one of them spoke, and Jerry certainly didn't feel like talking. The lead they thought had been so important had fizzled out. They'd have to return to the Lower Basin and sit around another week until they could come back. Unfortunately, the company finances were just about depicted. They would need food and gas, if nothing else.

The heat was beating down into the canyon, shimmering gauzily over the heights and even reflecting from the water, Buck and Whitey, stared away their gear. They looked at Jerry. There was nothing he could do but nod. Buck started the engine. It throbbed erratically, then settled down into full-bodied humming.

"Cast loose," said Jerry to Whitey.

Scat barked sharply.

Whitey grinned. "We forgot to pull up the weighted diving line," he said. "Scat didn't forget."

"I thought he sat on a tack," said Buck.

Buck took the boat hook and reached out for the buoy that floated on the surface with the diving line below it. He hooked the buoy and pulled it toward him, gripped it and started to pull it into the boat. The line tightened, sending off a shower of fine spray.

"Give it a yank!" said Whitey.

Buck pulled it again. The line was caught fast. "Wouldn't you know it," he growled.

"Let me help Muscles," said Whitey.

The two of them tugged and pulled. No use.

"I'll go down," said Jerry. "You two characters have done more than your share underwater today." He shut off the motor and let himself down into the water. He surfaced-dived, caught the taut knotted line and pulled himself down, hand over hand until he reached the murky bottom. The buoy weight was beneath drifted sand and mud. He pulled at it but could not free it. He was just about to go up for a knife to cut the line free when he felt something hard resting firmly against one side of the weight. He rubbed at it. It felt like metal. His lungs were about to burst, so he shot to the surface to draw in fresh air.

"Well?" said Buck.

"It's stuck beneath something. Give me a knife."

Buck handed Jerry a knife and Jerry went down again. He gripped the line just above the weight and began to saw at the line. It was then he noticed what was holding the weight fast. It was a sheet of metal, partly covered with wood, seemingly anchored in the sand and mud at each side of the weight. He scraped away at the metal with his knife. A flat, riveted surface showed. He let himself rise to the surface again and held on to *Huntress*.

"Give me a mask," he said.

He adjusted the mask and went down for the third time. He managed to clear the riveted metal surface, feeling along each end of it, finding another metal surface at right angles to the ends of the flat surface, but the right-angle pieces were curved and then rolled over at the top for strength. He passed his hands along each side until his hands met at a rounded boss of metal and he knew then and there he was in contact with the bow of a metal boat. Aluminum in all probability, and about thirteen to fifteen feet long at a guess, the larger part of it well buried beneath the mud and sand. This startling and unexpected find filled his mind as he shot to the surface and looked at the faces of his two friends.

"Buck," he said breathlessly. "Get on your diving gear again." He pulled himself into the boat and put on his flippers, readjusted his face mask, let his lungs fill again and again with the fresh air, then went down with Buck to the bottom, following the weighted line.

It was a matter of minutes, digging with their hands, to free the forward end of the boat from the sand and mud. The flat surface beneath which the weight had become caught was indeed a forward seat or thwart, well attached to the sides with angle metal and rivets. Jerry passed a hand beneath the seat, feeling for the flotation tank. His fingers found gashes cut into the tank, both forward and aft of the seat beneath which it was secured.

They rose to the surface to see the excited face of Whitey Cramer. "Well?" he demanded.

Jerry nodded breathlessly. "Boat," he said.

"Aluminum," gasped Buck. "Maybe fourteen feet long."

"Holes punctured in the flotation tank under the forward thwart," said Jerry. "Just like the ones in the tank we found among the driftwood."

Whitey hesitated. He swallowed. "Is it? Is it...?"

Jerry shrugged. "We don't know yet. The whole after end of it, maybe two-thirds of it, is buried beneath sand and mud. Take quite a while to free it."

Whitey looked up at the sun. "Well," he said, "we haven't much time."

Buck drew in a deep breath. "If we can free the goo from the sides near the stern, we might find the name."

Whitey shook his head. "Just take a look on either side of the bows," he said. "You'll find the registration number there. That ought to be enough to let you know if it is *Explorer*."

Buck shook his head. "Leave it to him," he said. "*I* was gonna dig out the whole blasted boat to find a name, and the little man here, *he* figures out the answer."

Jerry dived. The water was murky with whirling silt. He gripped his left hand under the coaming at the forward end of the sunken boat and passed his free hand over the flat metal where the registration numbers should be. He found them and his heart skipped a beat, for they were metal letters instead of the decalcomania type. He held his breath while he traced each of the letters, and when he reached the last letter, he tapped Buck on top of the head and jerked a thumb upward. They rose together up through the water and broke surface.

"Well?" said Whitey.

Jerry drew in a deep breath. "It's her all right," he said quietly.

"You're positive?" said Buck.

"Yes."

Buck looked about the cove. "The stuff we found on the shore must have come loose from her. Beats me how that punctured tank got up there. Unless it was punctured after it drifted ashore, and that doesn't make much sense."

"Puncturing the tanks, *in* or *out* of the boat, doesn't make sense," said *Jerry*.

"Now that we've found her," said Whitey, "what do we do next?"

Jerry looked at Buck. "Do you think we can free her of that mud and sand enough to find out what's in her?"

"Like what?" said Buck quietly.

They all looked at each other. There was no need for Buck to explain. Chuck Hunter and *Explorer* had vanished together. They had found *Explorer*. Was it possible that her owner had gone down with his boat? *That he was still in it?*

Suddenly the water seemed to have a chill in it,

arising from the murky depths below Jerry Hunter, and he knew he could not force himself to go down once more to the boat that lay there, more than half buried on the bottom.

Whitey looked up at the sun. "We can mark the place," he said. "That is, if you want to go home now."

"We'd better not leave a marker buoy floating here," said Buck.

Whitey shook his head. "We can take bearings on the shore," he said. "The cove isn't so big that we couldn't find the boat easily enough when we come back. All right, Jerry?"

Jerry stripped off his mask and pulled himself up into the boat. He dropped into a seat and removed his flippers. He was dead beat, and now that they had found the missing boat, something had gone out of the quest. Now that he was on the track of the mystery, he wasn't at all sure that he wanted to know the final answer.

Whitey took the bearings and jotted them down in a notebook. Buck started the motor, moved the boat closer to the marker buoy and cut it loose at the surface, letting the white nylon line float down to the bottom. It would help locate *Explorer* when they returned for the final work on her.

Huntress moved out of the cove at slow speed. It was then that Scat leaped up on a seat and looked back up the shadowed canyon, barking repeatedly until the canyon mouth was out of sight behind a huge shoulder of weathered rock.

Buck moved toward the center of the channel. There were no other boats in sight. He turned to starboard and increased the speed of the boat. It was a long way back to the marina in Lower Basin.

"One thing's for sure," said Whitey complacently, "this time the Rover Boys didn't spot us."

"Maybe they passed us half a dozen times and we didn't know it," said Buck.

"So?" said Whitey. "They don't know what we know. I'd sure like to know just what they're after."

"Quién sabe?" said Jerry. He looked back at the almost indistinguishable mouth of the cove where *Explorer* had lain submerged for the past three years. He was sure that the answer to the final mystery lay somewhere in or about that cove.

Chapter 7

There Are Things a Man Must Do

IT WAS THURSDAY EVENING, THE DAY BEFORE Jerry and his pals planned to return to the cove where they had found *Explorer*, when the blow fell. Jerry's father was finishing his newspaper in the living room when Jerry came in. Buck's pickup rattled off down the street.

"You're late," said Bill Hunter to Jerry.

"We had some things to do at school," said Jerry. "Then Ben Shoemaker had told me he had an extra prop somewhere around that would fit our motor. Said I could have it. I thought we should have an extra prop for *Huntress*."

"Good idea," said Bill Hunter. He folded the paper and placed it on the table. "Were you, by any chance, planning another weekend in the wilds of Lake Mead?"

"Yes, sir."

Bill Hunter nodded. "Well, you will probably be on the lake, but not for the weekend."

Jerry narrowed his eyes, wondering if his father had found out about the discovery of *Explorer*. Jerry had meant to tell him eventually, but not until the cove and adjacent territory had been well covered by the three searchers, Buck, Whitey, and himself.

"Did you want to use the boat?" asked Jerry.

"You know how I feel about *Huntress*," said his father. "Oh, I'll get over it in time, but I'm not ready yet. Fact is, I was in Las Vegas today on business and ran into Jim Bedloe. You remember him, I'm sure. He and your uncle had much the same interests, except that Jim did most of his exploring in an armchair. Jim and your uncle were pretty close for some years, although Jim is my age. Went to college with me in fact." He looked up at Jerry. "You remember he had a daughter about your age?"

Jerry grinned. "Yeh, skinny, freckle-faced, and noisy."

"Hmmm...well, she's changed, Jerry. I saw her yesterday. She said she and two of her friends were planning to come to Lake Mead for a two-day outing. They wanted to rent a boat, but I said that wasn't necessary. That they could use *Huntress*."

Jerry's heart sank within him. He opened and closed his mouth. "Yeh?" he said weakly.

"I know how you feel about the boat, so I said you and your two *amigos* would be more than glad to escort the three girls about the lake this weekend. You can take them out Saturday, bring them back here, then take them out again Sunday."

Jerry smiled wanly. "They could use Ben Shoemaker's boat, Dad. It's Fiberglas and has a good motor."

"The girls don't know the lake, Jerry."

Jerry thought of waiting yet another week before he and his friends could take *Huntress* far up the Colorado to continue their quest.

Bill Hunter stood up. "The girls will be here Saturday morning about nine, as far as I know. Maybe you'd better get the boat cleaned up a bit. It's a little messy."

"It's just our gear in there, sir."

His father's gray eyes studied Jerry closely. "Yes," he said quietly. It was as though he suspected that Jerry was holding something back from him. Maybe he had invited the girls to come out to the lake for an outing to keep Jerry and his friends from their quest. "Well, clean it up," he continued. He took out his wallet. "You'll likely need some cash. You always do." He handed Jerry a twenty.

Jerry eyed the twenty after his father had left the room. He knew right then and there that his father expected him to show the three Las Vegas girls a good time. Any other time it would have been all right. He thought of Linda Bedloe and the thought sent a chill through him. He'd have to be nice to her, of course. It wasn't the thought of taking a gremlin like Linda Bedloe out that really bothered him though. It was losing another weekend, when the trail was so hot. The boys had talked of nothing else but returning up the river all that week. Another cold feeling came over Jerry. Both of them were coming over that evening to work on the boat and study Chuck Hunter's books and maps. Jerry would have to tell *them* about the three girls from Las Vegas.

Jerry was cleaning out *Huntress* when he heard the truck halt in the street. He could hear the animated voices of Buck and Whitey. They were certainly looking forward to Friday afternoon and the trip up the lake.

Buck was first into the garage and he looked quickly about as he saw some of the gear strewed about the floor. "What's up?" he asked. "Restowing cargo, mate?"

Oh man, oh man, thought Jerry.

"Well?" demanded Buck.

Jerry turned. "We've got to clean out the boat," he said. Before they could shoot questions at him, he told them of the plans for the weekend.

"Count *me* out," said Buck. "I don't plan to spend this weekend entertaining some kookie girls from Las Vegas. You and Whitey can do the honors."

Whitey shook his head. "I'll help clean out the boat," he said. "That's as far as Ol' Whitey goes."

"It isn't as though it was forever," protested Jerry. "It's only a week's difference." Even as he said it, he felt a little sick inside. Only a week...

Whitey began to stow away the gear on the shelves at the side of the garage. Buck climbed into the boat and began to heave out the items that were not necessary for a social trip on the lake.

"We'll need a couple more life jackets," said Jerry desperately. "We only have four of them aboard."

"That's plenty for you and the three little maids from school," said Whitey.

"Look, fellas," protested Jerry. "It wasn't *my* idea."

There was no answer.

"Linda Bedloe's father was a good friend of Uncle Chuck," said Jerry. "We owe it to Uncle Chuck to be nice to her and her friends."

"He was your uncle," said Buck mercilessly. "Hey, Whitey, what'll we do this weekend?"

Whitey was wiping the sleek side of the boat. "You Dame it, *amigo*. I'm game for anything."

Jerry threw down an old shoe he had found in the bottom of the boat, beneath a seat. "All right," he said. "I won't ask you again. When we get done here, we can go study Uncle Chuck's maps and things."

"Fair enough," said Buck. "Now we're getting somewhere."

Jerry's mother was seated on the back patio. She looked up as the three boys walked toward the guest house. "Jerry," she said, "do any of you boys smoke?"

"You know I don't. Mother," said Jerry.

"I don't," said Buck. "No good for the wind. Can't play football and smoke at the same time."

Whitey smiled weakly. "I tried it. Found it stunted my growth and gave it up."

Mrs. Hunter held out something to Jerry. "I found this in the guest house this afternoon," she said.

Jerry took it from her hand, and for the third time that night a chill went through him. It was a little muslin sack with a drawstring, the kind in which Bull Durham tobacco is carried. He did not dare look at his two friends.

"Maybe it belonged to Uncle Chuck," said Jerry.

"He didn't smoke, Jerry, and besides, your friends would think I wasn't much of a housekeeper if I had left something like that lying around in the guest house for three years, wouldn't they?"

Jerry nodded. "It might have blown in," he said.

"I suppose so."

They walked to the guest house and, when Whitey had closed the door behind them, they all looked at the innocent appearing tobacco sack. Mingled thoughts raced through their minds.

"Maybe your father?" said Buck.

"No," said Jerry. "He smokes a pipe, and not very often at that." He looked at Whitey. "And it wasn't my mother, if that's what you're thinking!"

Whitey smiled sweetly. "Now what made you think I'd say a thing like that?"

"Maybe we're putting too much importance on a Bull Durham sack," said Buck.

"You got any other answers?" said Whitey. "Let's not kid ourselves, fellas. Whoever these characters are, they haven't given up."

Buck closed a big hand into a rocky looking fist. "What bothers me is that we've never really gotten a good look at them, except that one character in the boat. The one who came around the house. *He* smoked Bull Durham."

Jerry nodded. "Take a look around. Watch what you pick up. Maybe well find something else."

It was Whitey who found the screwdriver marks in the white paint of the bathroom window frame. Whoever had entered had slipped a screwdriver between the aluminum screen and the frame, then worked up the screen latch. After that he had pried up the window, which evidently had not been locked.

"Look at this," said Buck from the living room. Jerry and Whitey left the bathroom and saw Buck holding out a booklet. "Weren't there a map and some charts in the pocket at the back of this book?" he asked.

It was a sportsman's guide to Lake Mead and the Colorado River area, and within a pocket at the rear of it, had been a general map of the area and some detailed charts of the various channels and basins of the lake and river.

"Anything else missing?" asked Jerry.

Buck shrugged. "Not that I know of. If it was just a sneak thief, he'd have taken some of the goodies here. Some of those rifles are worth plenty. So is that camera on the shelf. Couple of those fishing reels are the best you can get. No, whoever it was wasn't looking for anything like that. He came for something specific. Like the map that was in here."

"You sure about the map?" asked Whitey.

"Yes."

Jerry walked over to a bookcase and picked up the missing map. "Here it is," he said.

"That blows that theory," said Whitey.

"No," said Jerry. "He wasn't interested in the map. He wanted the charts of the channels and basins. The map was too general."

"Beats the devil out of me," said Buck.

Jerry took the booklet from Buck. Something stirred in his memory. He had been looking through those missing charts during the week. He had been studying at the table and the booklet had been lying there. Idly he had begun to study the charts. Then a cold finger seemed to trace itself up the length of his spine. "Oh Lord," he said softly.

"What's the matter?" asked Buck.

Jerry placed the booklet on the table. "I was studying out here Tuesday night," he said. "I had a pencil in my hand and began to look through the charts in this booklet. I remember now that I drew a circle around the area in the God's Pocket vicinity, marking the cove where we found *Explorer*. I wasn't sure about the exact cove. Anyway, I drew the circle around about three of them as I recall."

Buck stared at Jerry. "You gone loco or something?"

Whitey whistled softly. "Man, you might just as well have made a sign and anchored it above the boat, with a long finger pointing down. X marks the spot!"

"I didn't mark the exact place," said Jerry, "because I wasn't sure myself. I could remember the cove by seeing it, but not on the chart."

"Maybe that's why the boys haven't been around," said Buck.

"They didn't show up last weekend," said Jerry. "That was *before* the chart was missing."

"How do we know they didn't show up last weekend?" said Whitey. "Remember that Jerry thought he saw something in that canyon, and Scat was excited about something up there too."

Buck rubbed his jaw. "So they find the boat," he said. "What then? They don't know any more than we do."

"No," said Whitey scornfully. "No, you big dope! But now they know *where* to look!"

Jerry nodded. "But for what?" he said, almost as though to himself. "Why do they want to find out what happened to Uncle Chuck? What had he found, or what was he looking for? They either want what he was looking for, or maybe Uncle Chuck, if he is dead, has something on his body they want. Like a chart or map or something. Something that will show them what it is, and where it is, whatever *it* was."

"Man," said Buck. "We ought to get back there as quick as we can!"

"No go," said Jerry.

"You mean you're going to take those three silly girls out this weekend?"

"It's that or my father will start asking questions. We can't lie to him, and, furthermore, I don't want to lie to him, but if he finds out what we know, the authorities will surely take an interest in what we've found."

Buck shrugged. He walked to the door. "Well, I might as well go home. See you around, Jerry."

Jerry waved a hand. It hurt him to think that Buck felt the way he did, but there was nothing Jerry could do about it.

Whitey rubbed the top of Jerry's head. "See you tomorrow," he said.

"Yeh," said Jerry. He heard the door close behind Whitey. Now that he was alone, the night seemed to draw in closer, as though there were something in the outer darkness that was watching and listening.

He thought of *Explorer* half buried in the mud and sand at the bottom of the unnamed cove. Maybe Uncle Chuck was still in it. Maybe whatever those three men were looking for was on a chart or map, still in the boat, or perhaps on the body of Uncle Chuck. Yet, somehow, his mind refused to accept the fact that Uncle Chuck was dead. Maybe it was a fixation; something that was true, but his mind would not let him believe. All that week he had thought about little else other than getting back to the cove. Buck, a skilled skin diver, had managed to borrow some scuba gear, but for that weekend only, and with it he would have been able to stay down on the bottom of the cove for quite some time.

Maybe he should make a clean breast of the whole thing and tell his father what they had found, and perhaps his father would give them permission to return to the cove to continue the search. Jerry had had the feeling for some time that his father suspected that the three friends weren't spending all that time on the lake just fishing and horsing around. He was far too shrewd for that, yet he had not given any indication that he thought Jerry and his two pals were doing anything else but playing around. Actually the authorities could do little more than the boys had done. They had found the lost boat. If Chuck Hunter was not in it, or near it, they'd merely write off his death was accidental and let it go at that.

Then, too, there was a streak of hardheaded stubbornness in Jerry Hunter. He and his pals had traced the trail of Chuck Hunter years after it had been made. It was cold to anyone else. It was their quest and theirs alone!

It was only a matter of two weeks before the three companions would be out of school, with a whole summer ahead of them to pursue the quest. In the fall they'd all be gone their separate ways Buck into the Navy, Whitey and Jerry to college. Time was running apace.

Jerry stood up, flicked out the lights, checked the windows and the rear door, then locked the front door and walked toward the house. He looked to the northwest, in the general area of the cove containing *Explorer* and his heart tugged within him.

He walked to the rear door of the house. "Linda Bedloe," he groaned. He shook his head. There are things a man must do. Duty called. He had no other choice.

Chapter 8

Three Little Maids from School

IT WAS AS LOVELY A JUNE DAY AS JERRY HUNTER had ever seen, and as the convertible moved down the long slope toward the marina, he could see the bright waters of the Lower Basin already dotted with boats, moving out from the marina. The distant humming of powerful motors drifted up the slope.

"It's lovely," said Linda Bedloe. She glanced sideways at Jerry. "Where is *Huntress?*"

"Dad and I brought her down yesterday evening and put her in the water, Linda," he said. "Just drive into the parking lot to the right of the road." He forced himself to take his eyes from her. It was as his father had said the night he had told Jerry about Linda and her two friends coming to the lake for a two-day holiday. *"Hmmm...well, she's changed, Jerry."* His father was never given to exaggeration, and this time he had outdone himself. Linda *had* changed. The metamorphosis from a skinny, freckled, noisy fifteen-year-old had been so great that Jerry had not recognized her when she drove up to the Hunter house that morning with her two girlfriends. A few of the freckles remained, dusting her upper checks and the bridge of her pert nose, but they added to, rather than detracted from, her appearance. The honey-colored hair and the clear gray eyes, that had a way of seeming to look right through a person, blended together into something quite different from what Jerry had expected.

Helene Squires leaned forward from the back seat. "I can hardly wait to get into the water," she said excitedly. She was taller than the other two girls, athletic looking, and vibrant with enthusiasm and life. Her titian hair was cut into a boyish hairdo that suited her very well.

"I'll stay on top of it," said Candy Kingman. "I like to look *at* water, not live *in* it."

She was the smallest of the trio, dark-haired and petite, hardly more than five feet tall, a miniature doll, with wide, expressive eyes that were as blue as Lake Mead.

Linda turned into the parking area and stopped the car. As Jerry got out, he happened to notice a battered, dusty pickup rattling down the road, raising a streamer of dust behind it. There wasn't any doubt in his mind about who was in the truck. Linda had passed it at a stoplight in Boulder City, and two pairs of eyes had bugged out at the sight of Jerry Hunter seated in the convertible, literally surrounded by feminine beauty, but there had been absolutely no recognition from Jerry, nor had he looked back as the convertible sped down the road toward the lake, despite the asthmatic wheezing of the pickup's horn.

Jerry carried two of the girls' cases, while Helene Squires carried hers, as they walked toward *Huntress*. Brakes squealed as the pickup came to a halt in a billowing of dust. Two doors opened and slammed shut.

Bill Hunter had managed to have *Huntress* moored

beside the marina pier. She bobbed gently in the swell. Jerry had to admit to himself she looked a lot better without the junk and odds and ends that usually cluttered up her cockpit when the three searchers were at work far up the lake.

Feet thudded on the pier as Jerry helped Linda into the boat, then Candy. Helene dropped lightly into the boat and took the cases from Jerry's hands. "Do you want me to help you with the other things from the car?" she asked.

"No need for that, ma'am," said Buck Lyon with a wide grin creasing his tanned face. "Now that *we're* here."

"Yeh," said Whitey. "The ol' crew of the ol' *Huntress* is here for duty, ma'am. Cap'n Hunter, sir! Reporting for duty, sir!"

Jerry looked out across the lake. "I could swear I heard voices in the distant wind," he said reflectively. "Voices of the long dead past. Of friends, now buried and almost forgotten. Old friends. Cherished friends. Trusted friends who'd never let a pal down. No more. No more..."

"You don't suppose he means us," said Buck to Whitey.

"Certainly not."

"The little one is cute," said Helene Squires.

Whitey smiled.

"The big one is, well, he *is* big," said Candy doubtfully. Her eyes seemed to be twice as large as they really were.

Buck Lyon looked as though he had been struck by a harpoon. "Six feet even," he said. "Hundred and eighty pounds."

"And no brains," said Jerry dryly.

"Me," said Whitey. "I'm five feet eight. 'Bout one hundred and forty."

"He gained two inches and ten pounds in two days," said Jerry.

"He's *cute!*" said Helene.

Linda looked at Jerry. "I thought you said your two boy friends were too busy to go out with us today," she said.

There was a long moment of silence.

Bock looked at Jerry and the look reminded Jerry of how Scat could look when food was being prepared or served.

"Let me help you stow those dungs," said Whitey. He looked at Jerry. "Permission to come aboard, sir?"

Jerry yawned. "Permission granted," he said.

Buck grinned again. "Let's go get the rest of the stuff, Jerry." he said.

Jerry nodded. He walked with Buck toward the convertible.

"Man," said Bock. "What a dirty trick! If me and Whitey hadn't happened to see you, you and those three dolls would have had a pretty lonely afternoon out there on the lake." He eyed Jerry suspiciously. "I believe you knew all the time what they looked like."

Jerry inspected his fingernails. "Count *me* out," he said, imitating Buck's voice on the night Jerry had told him about the girls coming for the weekend. "I don't plan to spend this weekend entertaining some kookie girls from Las Vegas. You and Whitey can do the honors."

Buck wasn't paying any attention to Jerry. "Don't look now," he said out of the corner of his mouth, "but when we get to the car, look toward the far side of the parking lot."

Jerry unlocked the trunk of the convertible and began to take out food hampers and other necessities for the day's outing. He flicked a glance toward the far side of the parking lot. Two men stood beside a sedan, watching Jerry and Buck.

"I saw them up at the road junction," said Buck. "They followed you and the girls down here. I guess they didn't see me and Whitey behind them."

"So? How do we know who they are?"

Buck shrugged. "I can feel 'em, man!"

They carried the things to the boat. Jerry glanced back toward the parking lot. The sedan was still there, but the two men were gone. Jerry shrugged. Buck had been building things up in his mind.

Jerry took *Huntress* out past the pier and set a course for Sentinel Island. Now and then he looked back, but there were so many boats in the mooring and moving about that it was hard to tell if they were being followed.

Buck looked at Whitey. "Saw two of our friends back there," he said. "Lost sight of 'em though."

Whitey nodded. He glanced at Jerry. "Where we heading, Skipper?"

"I thought we would head for Boulder Canyon. We can decide where to go when we pass through it."

"How about Overton Arm?" said Whitey. "We haven't been up there this year yet."

The message was clear enough. If they were going to be followed, and they didn't intend to go to the area where they had found *Explorer*, they could lead the two characters behind them on a wild goose chase. Besides, thought Jerry, they had the girls with them and they might as well make a day out of it.

"Fortification Mountain," said Linda Bedloe. She was

looking toward the huge shape of the flat-topped mountain that dominated the Lower Basin of Lake Mead.

"Yes," said Jerry.

"Those are the Black Mountains beyond it."

Jerry looked quickly at her. "Yes." She seemed to know something about the features of the area. He had been through similar experiences before. Some girls had a trick of learning a little bit about what a fellow was interested in, then playing it to the limit to hook him. That wasn't for Jerry Hunter.

He knew both his buddies were keeping a lookout for nearby boats. At least he hoped they were, for the two of them were getting on famously with the two girls. He glanced into the rearview mirror and saw the face of Buck, looking down at Candy Kingman like a huge Saint Bernard watching a kitten. "Oh Lord," said Jerry aloud.

"What's the matter?" asked Linda.

"Nothing," he said. "Thought I forgot something for a minute." He looked back at Whitey. Whitey was talking with Helene Squires. It seemed as though neither one of his *crew* was much interested in anything outside of the cockpit of *Huntress,* and the two girls in it.

Now and then he looked about the boat. There were plenty of other boats not too far from them. He knew some of them and others were strange to him, but as yet none of them seemed interested in the course *Huntress* was taking beyond Sentinel Island.

"Swallow Cove and Callville Bay," said Linda, pointing out the two areas as *Huntress* cruised toward Boulder Canyon.

She must have a map engraved in her memory, thought Jerry.

Buck came forward and looked at the speed indicator. He looked at Jerry out of the corner of his eye when he was sure Linda was looking the other way and moved his head in the direction of the stern. Then Buck returned to Candy. Jerry looked back. A boat was coming up fast astern, throwing up a rooster tail. It was about a twenty- or twenty-two-footer, with twin engines and a small cabin with a navy type top over the forward end of the wide cockpit. An odd feeling came over Jerry. It might be the boat that had been following them a couple of weeks ago. Then, too, those two characters in the parking lot had seemed pretty well interested in Jerry and Buck. They had followed the convertible down to the lake.

Buck uncased the field glasses and stood up in the stern. "Forgot to see if the storm flags might be flying," he said. A few moments later he cased the glasses, and when he caught Jerry's eye, he nodded. The silent message was plain enough.

There wasn't any doubt that the other boat had much more power than *Huntress*, although it was possible that *Huntress*, with her well-designed hull and the addition of a bottom pad and side stabilizers, might just hold her own with the oncoming boat, despite the difference in horsepower. Jerry eased back on the throttle, hoping that the other boat would pass them, but as he did so the boat veered off and fled away from them, spreading a creamy wake behind its thrashing twin propellers.

Whitey was now taking an interest in the other boat. "Awful lot of power on that baby," he said. "She's plan-ning, but notice how her stern squats in the water? She's digging in far too much."

"How interesting," said Helene Squires. She beamed at Whitey.

Whitey seemed to grow a little in stature. "Now, if they changed the tilt angle of those motors, and made a few other changes, she might be as fast as *Huntress*."

"Tilt angle or not," said Buck quietly, "she still has the legs on us."

Jerry increased the speed of *Huntress* and as she began to plane, he looked back toward the other boat. It had turned again and was bounding across the wake of *Huntress*, throwing up sheets of spray from her sleek bows as she hit the rougher waters. Once the other boat cleared the wake, she seemed to fly across the smoother water, but it was as Whitey had observed; with all her power, she was digging in too much at the stern, throwing up wake waves on each side so high that the tops of the motors were almost on a level with them. Of course, when the power was cut, the stern would rise, so there wasn't too much danger of the waves flowing in to swamp her. A little careless handling might do it.

"With those wake waves," said Jerry, "if she were ever stopped dead in the water, the wake would probably flow clear over the transom. I've seen those high-powered buckets do that many a time."

Huntress turned into high-walled Boulder Canyon and Jerry kept her at a steady cruising speed. It wasn't until they were at the other end of the canyon, with Boulder Wash opening to port, that they knew the other boat was coming along behind them.

Out in Virgin Basin, there were quite a few boats, though not a third as many as dotted Lower Basin. Neither Buck nor Whitey made any comment to Jerry as he turned to look back at them. Candy and Helene seemed unaware of what was going on, but when Jerry turned back to look ahead, he saw Linda watching him curiously.

He increased speed as they cleared the canyon mouth. "Where to?" he asked Linda.

"It doesn't matter to me."

Jerry was heading *Huntress* due east. Beyond Middle Point he'd have to make his decision, to turn left into Overton Arm, to turn right toward Bonelli Landing or Detrital Wash, or to continue east toward East Point and thence into the river channel again, heading up the channel.

As Middle Point showed clearly, he made his decision, turning to port to head for Middle Point and the wide mouth of Overton Arm. He didn't want to take any chances of being trapped in some isolated cove by those men in the boat behind them, providing, of course, they were the men Jerry suspected them to be. Jerry's chief concern was for the girls.

As he steered toward Overton Arm, he thought of the missing chart, the one he had idly marked the night he had been studying in the guest house. If those mysterious men had taken it, they'd know surely enough that whatever they were seeking wasn't up Overton Arm. There was no way for *Huntress* to come out of the arm without being seen, and if Jerry headed up channel, they'd be able to tail him. He looked back over his shoulder. The other boat was following in their wake, a quarter of a mile behind them, at about the same cruising speed. Jerry kept heading for the center of Overton Arm. When he was well into it, he saw that the other boat was slowing down, although still taking the same course.

The sun was at its zenith when *Huntress* reached the area in Overton Arm where dun-colored islands reared their heads above the sparkling waters. He headed for the Lower Narrows to the left of Ramshead Island and past the island to turn again toward mid channel. Buck caught Jerry's eye and shook his head. The strange boat was no longer following them.

"How about a swim?" said Helene Squires.

"Fair enough," said Jerry. He could see a few other boats in the area. He steered past Bighorn Island to a cove where he and his friends had done some swimming earlier that year. He grounded *Huntress* gently. In a moment Helene Squires was in the water, swimming with speed and grace, with a small but determined figure coming along behind her. Whitey Cramer would be game to the end.

"Candy?" said Buck.

Her eyes seemed bigger than ever. "I don't want to muss my hair, Buckie," she said.

Jerry could not look at Buck. *Buckie!* Oh Lord! Wait until Whitey heard that one.

Jerry and Linda swam easily out to a sun-drenched rock and climbed out on it. She looked up the arm. "We can't be far from the Valley of Fire," she said.

"About five or six miles," he said. "You seem to know a lot about Lake Mead."

She smiled. "My father has all kinds of maps and charts of it," she said. "We used to come out here when I was a kid. Maybe you've forgotten those days? Several times we went out in *Huntress* with your uncle. You always seemed to have something else to do."

Jerry did not dare look at her. She had been quite different in those days. He had an uncomfortable feeling she knew why he hadn't ever gone with them.

"My father says there are Indian villages below the water," said Linda. She dabbled a foot in the water. She looked sideways at Jerry with those penetrating gray eyes of hers. "You're not much interested in them, though, are you?"

"Not much," he said.

"You and your two friends spend quite a bit of time out on the lake, don't you?"

"Yes."

"Fishing?"

"At times," he admitted. He saw Helene and Whitey racing back to *Huntress*. She had a good ten-foot lead on him. Trust Whitey to end up with an Amazon.

"You like the upper part of the lake best, don't you?" Linda asked.

"Yeh," he said. She was making him uncomfortable with her questions. "Ready to swim back?" he added.

They slipped into the water and swam back side by side. When they reached the shore, she looked up at the heat shimmering heights. "Sometimes I wish I were a boy," she said. "I'm a lot like my father. Interested in this area. You know. Lost mines. Indian relics. Old trails and so on."

"My dad said your father was more of an armchair adventurer. No offense, of course."

She laughed. "No! It's true. Your uncle was the one who went out to search. At that, though, I once heard him admit my father knew a lot more about this country than he did."

"That was quite a thing for Uncle Chuck to admit."

Her face sobered. "They never did find him, did they?"

He shook his head.

"I'm sorry about that."

He looked at her. "I don't believe he's dead. Does that surprise you?"

"No," she said quietly. "My father has said the same thing more than once."

He stared at her. "He has?"

She nodded. "Like the time he was supposedly seen in Fredonia, Arizona."

A strange feeling came over Jerry. "I never heard that rumor. Tell me about it."

She skipped a stone along the surface of the water. "Dad travels quite a bit. He was in Kanab last week and had to drive down to Fredonia on government business. When he was down there, he met an old friend of his. They got to talking about mutual acquaintances, and this friend said that he had seen Charles Hunter, or his double, late last summer, walking along a road not far from Pipe Spring. Dad's friend was driving the other way and was in a hurry, so he didn't stop. Later that day, about evening, he was walking past a grocery store in Fredonia, and saw the same man come out of the store, carrying a full sack of groceries. He called out to the man by name. He had known your uncle slightly, but the man vanished in the darkness. Funny thing. The man he saw was eating from a huge bag of potato chips. You know. The kind you buy for parties for dips and such."

Jerry again had the odd feeling. Uncle Chuck was a nut on potato chips, particularly the big kind you use for dips. Actually it didn't mean anything, for a great many people liked potato chips, including Jerry himself. Many a huge bag he had shared with Uncle Chuck in the old days. "Maybe he was mistaken," said Jerry.

"Oh, he knew your uncle, all right."

"Then why didn't he report it to the authorities? We would have been notified."

"Why should he?" she said. *"He didn't know your uncle Chuck had been missing for over two years at that time."*

Jerry looked across the arm toward the northeast, in the general direction of Fredonia. It was a small town in the Arizona Strip country, that part of Arizona between the Utah line on the north and the Grand Canyon on the south, historically and culturally linked with early Mormon Utah rather than with the rest of Arizona, from which it was separated by the gap of the Grand Canyon. Fredonia was a small town with a population hardly more than a half thousand people, if it had that many. South of Fredonia, Highway 89 trended south toward the Grand Canyon, one fork leading to the North Rim, the other east to cross the Colorado at Navajo Bridge.

Southwesterly from Fredonia was the lonely country, and the vast Shivwits Plateau. Beyond Shivwits Plateau was the channel of the Colorado. In that area, near God's Pocket, was where *Explorer* had been found. Charles Hunter had been a great hiker. A man who could cover rough country with the stamina of a mule and the agility of a mountain goat walking from the Shivwits Plateau area to Fredonia, for example, wouldn't be too difficult for a man like him. If it *had* been Uncle Chuck. If it was indeed him, *where had he come from? Where had he gone to?*

"Do you really think it was him?" asked Linda.

"I've never believed that he was dead."

"Maybe you should go to Fredonia and question the man who thinks it was your uncle Chuck he saw. There might be some clues he could give you. Something that might very well prove that it was your uncle."

"Or wasn't," said Jerry.

"It isn't so far to Fredonia," she said.

He shrugged. "Can't go today. Tomorrow we'll be out here on the lake again. Next week we'll be busy getting ready for graduation. I don't know how I could get away to do it."

She hesitated for a moment. "We wouldn't have to come out on the lake tomorrow," she said.

He shook his head. "I promised my father I'd entertain you. Not that I haven't enjoyed it," he said.

She smiled. "I've never been to Fredonia," she said. "Do you suppose that if we left here early enough, we could make it to Fredonia and back by tomorrow night?"

From then on, until *Huntress* headed back down Overton Arm to Boulder Canyon and Lower Basin, a great weight seemed to have been lifted from Jerry Hunter, and the day's outing was a tremendous success. It had been agreed that Buck and Whitey could use *Huntress* the next day to entertain Helene and Candy, while Jerry and Linda would leave at dawn for Fredonia. Buck and Whitey would take the two girls back to Las Vegas Sunday evening and pick up Jerry to bring him back to Boulder City. It was as simple as that.

Chapter 9

A Tale of Mormon Gold

IT WAS NOON WHEN JERRY STOPPED THE convertible in front of Andrew Tyson's house in Fredonia. Linda had fallen asleep beside Jerry, for they had left Boulder City before dawn. A lean-looking man was seated on the front porch of the house reading a newspaper. Jerry walked up to the house. "Mr. Andrew Tyson?" he said.

The man smiled. "The very same," he said. "What can I do for you, young man?"

Jerry looked back at the car. "That's Linda Bedloe asleep in the car, sir. She told me yesterday that her father had talked with you last week and that you had mentioned seeing Charles Hunter of Boulder City, here in Fredonia last year. I'm Jerry Hunter, Charles Hunter's nephew."

"That's right. I did see a man who resembled him. Jim told me he had been missing for about three years. I was quite surprised. I didn't know Charles Hunter too well. I could have been mistaken. I told Jim not to place too much stock in the fact that I had seen him or someone who looked like Charles Hunter."

"It has been assumed that he drowned in Lake Mead during a storm. I have reason to believe that might not be true."

Tyson rubbed his jaw. "I hate to think you might have come all the way over here on a wild goose chase. As I told you, it *might* have been him."

"But you saw him twice. Couldn't you have been sure it was him?"

"The first time I saw this man I was driving into Short Creek. Not far from Pipe Spring I saw a man step out of a ditch. I passed him, thought I knew him, slowed down and waved, then called out several times. Either the noise of the car drowned out my voice or he just ignored me. Later that day, just after dusk, I saw the same man coming from a grocery store here in Fredonia. I called out to him again, but he vanished in the darkness. Maybe it wasn't Charles Hunter after all. He did look different."

"In what way, sir?"

"Well, he was very thin, almost emaciated looking. His hair was long, and his beard was ragged. I don't remember Charles Hunter ever wearing a beard."

"He never did, Mr. Tyson."

"So you see, it is quite possible I made a mistake. Perhaps it wasn't him at all. When I saw Jim Bedloe here last week, I mentioned the incident. He then told me that Charles Hunter had been missing for three years. I was quite surprised. He said he didn't know whether to tell your father or not. I told him not to say anything until I could inquire around a bit to see if anyone else had seen this man I saw."

"And?"

Tyson shook his head. "Nothing. You must remember this is not a very populated section of Arizona. A man could walk the back country for days and never be seen. I'm sorry, young man."

Linda came from the car. "Hello, Mr. Tyson," she said with a smile. "I'm sorry I fell asleep. Jerry should have awakened me."

"Forget it, Linda," said Andrew Tyson. "How about some lunch? I live alone, but I'm not a bad cook."

"I'd like that, Mr. Tyson," she said.

He led them into the small and neat house, and while he prepared the lunch, he questioned Jerry about the particulars of Charles Hunter's disappearance. "What makes you think he's still alive?" he asked as he placed the food on the table.

"I don't really know," said Jerry. There was no need to tell Tyson about finding the boat. After all, it didn't prove anything about the death of Chuck Hunter, if he was dead. "I just had a hunch."

Tyson sat down with them. "Most everyone around here knows everybody else. Yet no one I talked with had seen a man answering the description of the man I had seen. If that man was Charles Hunter, where did he go? It isn't likely he's in any of the towns around here. If it was him, I'd say he's living in the wilds somewhere. But why? It doesn't make sense."

"Do you think a man could live in the country southwest of here and not be seen?" asked Linda.

"A good woodsman could," said their host. "There's plenty of game in there. Water. Shelter. Few people ever go in there."

"Uncle Chuck was as experienced in outdoor living as anyone I have ever known. Better, in fact," said Jerry.

"If he is alive," said Tyson, "why would he be hiding

out? Letting his relatives and friends think he was dead. Is there any reason for him doing that, Jerry?"

"Not that I know of."

"The man I saw might have been a tramp," said Tyson.

"Do you really think so?" asked Jerry.

Tyson rubbed his jaw. "I don't want to build up your hopes, Jerry, but I still think that man was Charles Hunter."

"What makes you think so?"

Tyson smiled. "I asked you why you thought he was still alive, and you said that it was a hunch. Say my belief that the man I saw was Charles Hunter is also a hunch. That's the best I can do for you."

"It's all very strange," said Linda. "Dad was very hesitant to talk about what you told him, Mister Tyson."

"I can see why." Andrew Tyson went back into the kitchen. "There was another man who thought the same way when I told him about seeing Charles Hunter, or his double. He said not to say anything until I was quite sure. Fat chance of that, because I doubt if I'll ever see that mysterious stranger again. Webb Macklin said he'd inquire about the country to see what he could find out."

"Who is Webb Macklin?" asked Linda as Tyson came back into the room.

Tyson sat down. "Sort of a man something like Charles Hunter was. Poking around in the back country. Hunting lost treasures and the like. I helped him some years ago when he was trying to track down a lost treasure story about the country southwest of here. Guess I didn't do him much good. He never said he had found anything. Come to think of it, I haven't seen Webb Macklin since I told him about seeing Charles Hunter."

Tyson laughed. "Mac is off somewhere on another of his wild goose chases, I suppose."

Jerry's head snapped up. "Mac?" he said.

Tyson nodded. "That's Webb's nickname."

"What does he look like, Mister Tyson?"

"Good-sized man. Rather large nose. Neatly trimmed mustache."

An icy feeling crawled through Jerry. "Does he live around here?"

"I don't think he calls any particular place home. Lived in Las Vegas for a time. Kingman. Henderson. Spent some time around Tucson. I think he was looking for the Lost Dutchman's Mine at that time. I always thought Mac would have been better off getting a steady job rather than chasing after lost treasures. Why? Do you know him?"

Jerry shook his head. Pieces of the puzzle were in his thoughts, but there was no place to fit them, not yet, at any rate. "I guess lie's a loner like my uncle was."

Tyson shrugged. "There was another man here with him the last time I talked with him, when I told him about seeing someone who looked like your uncle. Fella by the name of Siskin or something like that. Tough looking character. Looked like a miner or construction worker. Big and rugged."

Later, when they had finished eating, Jerry thanked Andrew Tyson, saying they had a long way to go to get back to Las Vegas before it was too late. "By the way," he added, "are there any roads southwest of here that lead toward the Shivwits Plateau?"

"A few. Bad though. I wouldn't try any of them with that car you have out there. There are a few ranches in that area. Very isolated. Seems to me, if you wanted to get into that country, you'd be better off to take that boat of yours and go up the Colorado and then leg it in."

Linda looked at Jerry. "I think that's a fine idea."

Jerry did not dare look at her; those eyes of hers had a way of probing right into a man's mind. "Mister Tyson," he said quickly, "you said you had been helping Webb Macklin with information about a lost treasure somewhere southwest of here. Could you tell me about that?"

"No reason I can't, seeing as it's more or less public domain. Back in the '80s, a shipment of gold bullion was lost somewhere between Kingman, Arizona, and Saint George, Utah. The bullion belonged to the Mormon Church and had been entrusted to some of their people for delivery to Salt Lake City. The party crossed the Colorado at Pierce's Ferry, then started through the Grand Wash area, heading for Saint George. They never got there. Just vanished. Eight or nine men, horses, mules, and gold. Poof! Just like that. To this day, about eighty years later, no trace has ever been found of the party or the gold. They left Pierce's Ferry, crossed the Colorado, and were last seen by the ferryman heading into the wilderness."

Jerry nodded. Pierce's Ferry wasn't too far from God's Pocket, where he and his friends had found *Explorer,* and that wasn't far from Grand Wash. Mormon gold! "How much gold was missing?" he said.

"Church records indicate it was in the neighborhood of a hundred thousand dollars. Quite likely an exaggeration."

Linda whistled softly. "Dad mentioned that lost Mormon gold once or twice, but he never said how much it amounted to."

"What do you think happened to it, sir?" asked Jerry.

"Who knows? Bandits might have ambushed the

party, killed them all, hidden the bodies, and taken off with the gold. Indians might have slaughtered them and dumped the gold somewhere in the area. It was of no use to them. My personal opinion is that it is somewhere beneath the waters of the Colorado since it was dammed, lost forever."

They said goodbye to Andrew Tyson and drove out from Fredonia, this time taking the road that trended southwesterly from the little town, past Shiprock and through the Kaibab Indian Reservation and Pipe Spring National Monument. Before the road turned north beyond Cedar Ridge, Jerry stopped the car to look southwest toward the Shivwits Plateau country. Somewhere in that hazy wilderness was the answer to the mystery of Charles Hunter. Much of it was still primitive, almost as it had been hundreds, even thousands of years ago, isolated and comparatively alone. Even as he looked across that lonely country he could see the vaporous trails of jets from the Air Force field at Las Vegas hanging in milky whorls against the cobalt sky, over a country that was almost as unchanged as it had been before the coming of the white man.

They stopped in Saint George for a malted, then drove on, making good time, and their conversation wasn't always about the mystery of Charles Hunter.

It was dark long before they neared Las Vegas. Jerry looked at Linda. "I wish you'd keep the information we learned today to yourself," he said.

"We didn't learn much, Jerry. Or did Mister Tyson say something that helped you more than I realized?"

"Well," he admitted, "there was a clue or two in what he said."

"But you don't want to tell me?"

"Not yet," he said.

"Was it about that lost Mormon gold?"

"Partly."

She leaned her head back on the seat. "Dad says he thinks it's somewhere in Lost Canyon."

It was a good thing there was no traffic at that moment for Jerry moved so suddenly the car swerved over the dividing line into the opposite lane. "Lost Canyon?" he said after he had the car under control.

"What startled you?" she said.

"Jackrabbit," he said quickly. He did not dare look at her. "Tell me about Lost Canyon."

"I don't remember too much. It seems to me your uncle and my father were talking about such a place not too long before your uncle disappeared. It's somewhere across the Colorado from Pierce's Ferry, further upstream from where the ferry landed on the north bank of the river between the Shivwits and Sanup Plateaus."

"Just *somewhere*? That's a lot of country over there, Linda."

"Dad said you could reach it from the God's Pocket area. He said you could tell that it was Lost Canyon because of the old Indian ruins in it. It isn't easy to find according to him."

"Why does your father think the treasure is in Lost Canyon?"

"Your uncle told him, Jerry. You know how he was always poking into the back areas. Dad thinks your uncle knew something more than he would admit. He wanted my father to go in there with him, but Dad likes to talk about such adventures, rather than experience them. He told your uncle to go ahead and scout Lost Canyon, and if he found anything, Dad said he'd give him a hand with it, but that he wouldn't expect a share of any treasure.

Frankly, I think Dad had little faith in the lost bullion story."

"You mean he doesn't believe it?"

"He believes it all right, it's just that he doesn't think it will ever be found."

Jerry was pretty quiet until they reached the street where Linda lived. "I wish your dad was home," he said. "I'd like to ask him about Lost Canyon."

She looked at him. "I've told you all he knows, Jerry. It does exist, though a great many people doubt it. I suppose because it's so well hidden."

"Yeh," he said quietly.

Buck's pickup was parked in front of Candy Kingman's home a few doors away from Linda's house. Jerry walked up to the front door of Linda's house with her. "Graduation is next week," he said.

"*I know.*"

He looked down at her. "I can get tickets for the prom," he said.

"*You haven't* asked anyone?"

"I am now," he said.

"You know the answer," she said. She reached up and drew his face down to hers, kissing him lightly. "I hope you find Lost Canyon, Jerry," she said. "Thanks for a lovely time. Good night."

"I'll call you tomorrow," he said.

He walked down the street and saw Buck and Whitey standing beside the truck. They got into the pickup and headed out of Las Vegas for Boulder City, while Jerry told them of what he had learned. "Anything happen while I was gone?" he asked.

"Quiet as the grave," said Buck.

"Don't say that!" protested Whitey. He looked at

Jerry. "We had a fine time explaining to your mother where you and Linda were, Jerry."

"I didn't want my folks to know. They'll know soon enough."

"Then it's up the Colorado next weekend?" said Buck.

Jerry hesitated. "Well, I'm not sure," he said.

"What do you mean?" asked Whitey in surprise. "This is what we've been waiting for! We'll be out of school. All the time in the world. The sooner we get out there the better, eh, Buck?"

"Yeh," said Buck.

Something in his tone made Jerry look quickly at him. "What's bothering you?" he asked.

Buck reddened. "Well, Candy sort of asked me to take her to the prom. What else could I do?"

"Oh Lord!" said Whitey. He rolled his eyes upward.

Half a mile sped past.

Jerry swallowed. "I asked Linda to go," he said. "She accepted."

Half a mile shot past in the darkness. Buck and Jerry dared not look at Whitey.

Whitey shifted in his seat. "Helene told me I was going to take her," he said at last.

Jerry laughed. "I guess Lost Canyon can wait until after the prom. It's been there a long time."

"And lost a long time," said Buck. "It didn't get its name for nothing."

Whitey looked at Jerry. "Do you think Mr. Tyson really saw your uncle, Jerry?"

"I want to believe it," said Jerry.

"Better not place too much stock in it," said Buck. "It's better not to believe that it was him, than to believe it and find out it wasn't."

"Gives you an eerie feeling," said Whitey. "Maybe it was a ghost."

"Eating potato chips?" said Buck.

Jerry did not speak. Somewhere in the brooding darkness beyond the Colorado was the answer to a three-year mystery. He wasn't sure about finding out what happened to Charles Hunter; he was sure that he was committed to the search until he found the answer.

Chapter 10

The Canyon Awaits

IT WAS DARK WHEN THE PICKUP CAME TO A HALT in the parking lot at the marina. Not even a trace of the false dawn showed in the eastern sky. A cold wind blew across Lake Mead, rippling the dark waters. The steady splashing of water came from the moored boats and from the pier as the wavelets lapped against them.

Buck Lyon got out of the pickup and looked about the parking lot. There wasn't a soul in sight. A half dozen parked cars were there, but there was no one in any of them. Jerry shivered a little in the cold wind. Without a word he grabbed some of the gear in the back of the truck and started down toward the pier, followed by Whitey, laden down with gear as well. Jerry placed the gear in a pram that was on the shore. It belonged to Ben Shoemaker, and he always let Jerry use it when he needed it Whitey placed his load in the boat, then helped Jerry shove it into the water. Whitey hurried back to the truck.

Jerry pulled out to *Huntress* and fastened the painter in the pram to one of her cleats. He swiftly unloaded the pram into the bigger boat, then went forward to cast loose from the mooring buoy. He *picked* up a long paddle and as *Huntress* drifted toward the shore, he helped a little paddling and steering with the blade. She grounded and Whitey waded in to grip her bow line. With the help of Buck, they pulled the bows further up on the shore. Whitey placed Scat in the cockpit. It was only a matter of minutes before finishing loading the boat. Whitey took the pram to where they had found it, then returned to *Huntress*. Buck and Whitey shoved her into the water, then clambered aboard as she swung around into the wind.

Jerry looked along the darkened shore. Not a sound of anyone. It was almost as though the entire area were empty of humans.

They paddled the boat beyond the mooring area and, once free of it, the wind shifted and began to drift them further out. While she was drifting, they stowed their gear. There was a lot of it, for the boys had a whole week ahead of them, financed by the parents of all three in recognition of their graduation. It was the only thing they had wanted. All of them had been dead broke after the prom. It had been worth it.

The lake was dark and rather uninviting. Buck looked at Jerry. "We're going to have to start the motor sometime, Commodore," he said in a low voice.

Jerry uncased the glasses and focused them on the shore. Still no sign of life. Maybe they had been too suspicious. "Okay, engine room," he said over his shoulder. "Kick her over."

The motor punched into life, throbbing erratically. The noise of it seemed to bounce back from the distant heights. Sound carries a great distance over water. Jerry walked forward to the wheel and dropped into the seat.

He switched on the lights, then eased the throttle forward and *Huntress* surged ahead. As soon as the motor had warmed up and she was far enough out from the shore, Jerry gave her more and more speed, until she was planing like a thing alive, throwing sheets of ghostly looking spray from her bows. Now and then the cold spray touched Jerry's face.

Whitey opened the bigger of the three thermos jugs they had and poured steaming hot coffee for the crew. He gave Scat a Milk bone to chew on, then took the field glasses to look back toward the marina.

Buck dropped into the seat beside Jerry. "She's a thoroughbred," he said.

"Who? Candy?"

Buck grinned. "Sure. She is too, but I was talking about *Huntress.*"

Always in darkness a body of water seems much bigger than it really is, and conversely, a boat seems much smaller. *Huntress* bored a hole through the thick darkness, intent on her business, and Jerry's heart warmed to her. It was almost as though she knew what was ahead of them. This time Jerry and his friends were determined to solve the mystery of Charles Hunter. In a matter of several months the trio would be broken up and *Huntress* would no longer be their home away from home. *She knew,* thought Jerry.

"Nothing," said Whitey. "Maybe they've given up, or we really gave them the slip. Haven't seen hide nor hair of any of them."

Jerry said nothing. A hundred thousand dollars in gold bullion was the magnet that drew those three men after Jerry and his friends. They'd hardly give up that easily.

They could see the lighted marker on Beacon Rock as

they passed Burro Point to starboard. It seemed a long way off in the thick darkness.

By the time they reached Beacon Rock the first pewter traces of the false dawn showed in the eastern skies above the wolf-fanged mountains. Minutes later they were in the dark trough of Boulder Canyon with the throbbing of the motor slamming back and forth between the towering walls.

The dawn was lighting the east when they left Boulder Canyon and headed across Virgin Basin toward the distant river channel about nine miles away as the crow flies.

Not a boat light showed on the vastness of the basin. The winking light on East Point guided them across the dark waters. Jerry kept the boat at a steady cruising speed. He wanted to reach the channel before the basin was fully lit by the day. Now and then he looked back but there wasn't a thing to see other than the dark water, with the wide, creamy V of the boat's wake spreading across it, and the towering heights surrounding the basin. Maybe Whitey was right at that. Maybe they had given up. It was going to be tough enough and rough enough as it was without competing with such characters. The bullion drew them on; it was Charles Hunter that drew the boys on.

The full light of day was flooding the country when *Huntress* passed Temple Bar Landing to starboard. Jerry now cut her down to a slower cruising speed to let Whitey get his galley work started and when they passed Salt Springs Wash heading for the mouth of Virgin Canyon, the odor of bacon and eggs rose from the wide cockpit of the boat to mingle with the exhaust fumes of the engine.

They passed an outboard heading down channel,

receiving a cheery greeting and a wave of the hand from the two men in it. They saw a number of boats moored in Salt Springs Wash. An early morning fisherman was trying his luck in Gregg Hideout. Virgin Canyon was empty of boats. The sun was flooding bright light down in Gregg Basin when *Huntress* entered it. Here and there along the length of the wide basin boats were moored, but none of them looked like cither of the boats that the boys were interested in. It was getting to be a puzzle in the mind of Jerry Hunter.

Whitey cleaned up the galley with the help of Buck and Scat, of course. He was handier than a garbage disposal. The things he could not eat were placed in the litter box to be disposed of in a suitable place for waste. Whitey took up his job as lookout with the field glasses, but there was nothing to alert them. A few boats here and there. A lone hawk hanging in the clear sky. A puff of cloud showing its whiteness beyond the mountains. A drifting log. The rippling water and the looming heights. Nothing to alarm them.

Buck filled a coffee cup for Jerry. "Beats the devil out of me," he said.

"I still think we gave them the slip," said Whitey.

"I wouldn't bet on it," said Jerry. He sipped his coffee, steering with one hand, eyeing each distant boat, each cove and beach they passed. Nothing.

The motor echoed steadily through Iceberg Canyon and not a boat was in it. Driftwood Cove was empty. Rattlesnake Cove held a big inboard cruiser, with the side curtains drawn and not a sign of life about it. When the boat turned into the channel that led into Grand Wash Canyon not a boat or human was to be seen. Jerry cut the speed of the boat and plowed slowly against the strong current, just keeping steerageway on the boat.

They slowly rounded a sharp-toothed point where they had a long view of the upper river. Nothing but the sun sparkling from the water and the rustling of tamarisks along the shore.

Whitey studied each cove and point, then the snaggletooth heights. He shook his head.

Jerry let *Huntress* turn with the current, which carried her past a mass of slowly revolving driftwood, then increased the speed until they rounded a point. He slowed down again, then stopped the motor, and as *Huntress* drifted down toward God's Pocket the three boys kept an eagle eye out for boats or humans. After the roaring of the motor, it seemed unnaturally quiet. The wind moaned through the narrows. The water splashed against rock and shore.

A few strokes with the paddles turned the boat into the cove where they had found *Explorer*. She drifted slowly behind the rock shoulder that concealed the rather large, though narrow cove. A hollow, tinkling sound came from the wavelets lapping into rock crevices.

There was no sunlight as yet in the cove and the mouth of the canyon that led up into the mysterious unknown was still shrouded in shadows. A chill wind flowed down it to fill the cove.

"Cheerful place," grunted Buck as he picked up the coiled mooring line and stepped up on the forward deck. *Huntress* drifted toward the wide rock ledge that overhung the water. Buck stepped onto the ledge and made the line fast as the others fended off, then hung life jackets over the side to keep the boat from chafing, although there was hardly any current in the cove.

Jerry looked down at the dark waters. Somewhere down there was *Explorer*, and perhaps the bones of his uncle. In the back of his mind was the belief, and hope, that it was actually Charles Hunter who had been seen in Fredonia.

"Orders, Commodore," said Whitey.

Jerry turned. "Same as before. Whitey, you stand guard with Scat. Scat, you let us know if Whitey smells anything. He has a good nose, even if he isn't too bright."

"Whurf," said Whitey. He wrinkled his nose and tilted his head to one side in exact imitation of his dog.

Buck was already getting into his skin-diving gear. There was never a waste of time with Buck. Cold water or warm water made no difference to him. Minutes later he was over the side, plunging deep to find the white nylon line they had left to mark the location of the wreck.

Whitey shivered. "No sense and no feeling," he said.

Buck rose to the surface with the line in his hand. Jerry made it fast to the buoy. "She's still down there," said Buck.

Jerry thrust a sheathed knife beneath his belt and went over the side. The water was cold but invigorating. He gripped the line and pulled himself down hand over hand until his feet touched the wreck. A moment later he felt Buck touch him. They had made their plan of operation before they had left Boulder City that day.

Jerry worked steadily, freeing mud, silt, and rock from one side of the boat while Buck worked along the other side. They worked slowly, fanning away the silt that rose from the disturbed bottom, so that the water would not become too clouded. As it was, it was almost impossible to see much.

Buck touched Jerry on the shoulder and jerked a thumb upward. They rose together. The sun was beginning to shine down into the far side of the cove.

"Quiet as the grave," said Whitey. "Three gone men on the Dead Man's Chest. Yo ho ho and a bottle of cleaning fluid."

Buck groaned. "Wait until we get underwater at least, will you, Milburn?"

"All right, Buckie," said Whitey with a sweet smile of resignation.

They went down several more times and worked steadily until they had the boat cleared to the middle thwart, then rose to the surface again for rest and air.

"Nothing doing up here," said Whitey. "How about me going down?"

"Pretty soon," said Jerry. He wanted to work until he found something conclusive. Buck could outwork the both of them underwater so he could work with each of the others in turn. He and Jerry dived again.

The middle thwart had no flotation tank beneath it. It was obvious that the flotation tank they had found on the shore had somehow become detached from under the seat, for the seat was loose at one end and a heavy rock had fallen on it. Buck found a small thermos bottle under the seat and, when they surfaced and cleaned it off, Jerry was quite sure it had belonged to his uncle. Buck worked off the cap and poured a muddy-looking liquid from the thermos into a tin can.

Whitey sniffed the liquid. "Coffee," he said.

It was noon before the two divers halted their work. They had cleaned out most of the forward half of the boat, finding various odds and ends, some of which gave Jerry quite a turn. A rusted fishing reel. A wad of hooks welded together by rust. A soaked tennis shoe. A tangled mess of monofilament fishing line. There was nothing, though, that gave them a clue to Charles Hunter.

Neither boy was hungry, and they dived after an

hour's rest, working steadily until they had cleared the portion of the interior aft of the middle thwart. It was Buck who unearthed the outboard motor's gas tank and horsed it to the surface. It had filled with water from a rough gash in the side.

The sun was now pouring its heat and fight into the cove and even the canyon looked fairly cheerful. Heat waves arose, shimmering and dancing, from the heights overlooking the cove and canyon. The intense light brought out the fantastic rock coloring in strong relief, and the rocks seemed to change their hue with the shifting of the lights and shadows that played across them.

"I'll spell you," said Whitey to Jerry.

"Thanks, Whitey, but I want to keep on."

Whitey did not press him. He knew how Jerry felt.

In an hour they knew that, wherever Charles Hunter was, he wasn't within the wreck of his boat. The motor was still clamped to the transom and was undamaged except for the long immersion it had suffered. There was no need to bring it to the surface. They found other odds and ends within the boat, but not a clue to the disappearance of Charles Hunter.

The last thing they did was to work along the sides and stern of the boat, trying to find the body, a gruesome but necessary task, and Whitey dived for a time to help them. If Charles Hunter lay beneath the dark waters of the cove, he was not within ten feet of the wrecked boat.

The three of them surfaced for the last time that day, thoroughly beat, and crawled into *Huntress*. It was still early afternoon and very hot.

"I'm beginning to think that Chuck Hunter never died in the lake or the river," said Buck wearily.

Whitey looked toward the canyon mouth. "Maybe up there," he said quietly.

Jerry lay back against the side of the boat and looked up the canyon. "A man could hardly live long in that country unless he was an expert in living outdoors."

"So?" said Buck.

Jerry glanced at him. "Did you notice one thing about *Explorer*? There wasn't any of the camping and outdoors gear that Uncle Chuck usually carried in it. He could have lived for weeks, months, even years using that gear."

Buck nodded. "Yeh," he said softly.

Whitey rubbed his jaw. "Could have drifted off or been washed away."

"All of it?" said Buck.

"Maybe it's lying around the bottom," said Whitey.

Jerry stood up. "No," he said thoughtfully. "The answer is somewhere up the canyon. I think *Explorer* was sunk on purpose, either by someone else, or *Uncle Chuck himself.*"

The two boys stared at Jerry. "Why?" they said together.

"To keep someone from finding it." Whitey shook his head. "Why would he do that? He knew how much your father and mother thought of him, not to mention you yourself, Jerry. Why would he vanish on purpose, letting his friends and relatives worry about him? It wasn't in his character, Jerry."

"I'll have to buy that," agreed Buck.

Jerry nodded. They were right. The fact still remained, though, that *Explorer* had been sunk on purpose, and that none of the camping gear that was usually carried in her was in her now. They were on the start of the trail that might, in time, solve the mystery of

Charles Hunter's disappearance, but there was a long and devious way to go.

"Then it's up the canyon tomorrow?" said Buck.

"Why not now?" said Jerry.

Whitey shook his head. "It's filled with heat now, Jerry, and both of you characters are tired out, though you'd never admit it, to me at least."

"I don't like to waste time," said Jerry stubbornly.

"There will be a new moon tonight," said Whitey.

Buck smiled. "Sometimes the little man comes out with a good idea. We'll have light and it will be cooler."

Whitey grinned weakly. Trust me to open my big month," he said. "I'm not too anxious to go up into that canyon, day or night."

"Why?" said Buck.

Whitey shivered a little. "Well, it sorta looks like it's just waiting for someone to wander up in there as if those high walls would close in behind you and you'd never get out again. There's something weird and uncanny about it. See how the light changes? How the walls seem to move back and forth?"

"Listen to him!" scoffed Buck.

All the same, it was as Whitey had said. Almost as though the twisted canyon beyond the cove were indeed waiting for something, or someone, like a beast of the jungle crouched in ambush, patiently waiting for its prey.

Jerry tore his mind from what Whitey had said. "We'll go up there when the moon rises," he said. "We came here to find out what happened to my uncle. We can't solve the mystery sitting here in the boat wondering what's up there, can we?"

Buck and Whitey shook their heads.

Jerry looked about the cove. "Meanwhile we had better figure out some way to conceal *Huntress* in case anybody comes poking in here while we're gone, and you know well enough who I'm talking about."

Busy as they were for the next few hours, now and then one of them, when he was sure the other two were not watching him, would glance quickly, and thoughtfully, up into the vague, shifting light of the shadowed canyon.

Chapter 11

A Cry in the Night

THE MOON TINTED THE EASTERN SKY WITH A
pale wash of ivory light as the three boys started up the
canyon with Scat trotting confidently along at the end of
a leash held in Whitey's hand. Fact of the matter is, Scat
was the only one of the party who felt any confidence
at all.

By a stroke of pure luck they had found that *Huntress*
fitted neatly beneath the wide rock ledge where they had
moored, after they had removed some loose rock and a
tree trunk that had long been wedged beneath it. At
night it would be almost impossible to see the boat, and
though it had gone against the grain of all three of them,
they had plastered her gleaming white side with mud
from the shore, so that no reflection of the moonlight on
the water of the cove would give away her position.

Jerry took the lead, working his way across a loose
deposit of detritus until he struck more solid ground.
From where he was standing, it seemed as though the
canyon ended in a blank wall, but a cool breeze was

drifting down the canyon, indicating that it continued beyond the seeming blankness ahead of the boys.

The canyon turned sharply to the right, continued for a hundred yards or so, then trended left in a loose S shape, and all the time the floor of it slanted steadily upward, so that the going was much harder than Jerry had anticipated. Here and there tangles of brush thrust up their wiry heads from crevices where thin earth pockets had formed. Despite the cooling effect of the night wind, there were still places where the sodden heat of the day was reluctantly being driven away by the coolness of the night.

Except for the dry whispering of the wind, it was very quiet, almost too quiet for normality. The silvery light of the moon was already washing the northern wall of the canyon at the upper part, picking out the serrated edge of the rim in sharp relief, and conversely, making the shadow pockets appear much darker and deeper than they really were.

The boys' boots grated softly on the hard ground and Scat's panting seemed louder than usual. The brush moved steadily back and forth, at times assuming odd and grotesque shapes that seemed vaguely menacing.

Higher and higher they climbed until the canyon turned sharply to the right again and the floor leveled off, though it was a tangled jungle of loose rock, talus, stunted trees, and thorny brush, which took time and care to get through.

Somewhere to the right of them, through almost impassable country, would be the deep trough of the Colorado River gorge, for here the river had driven its way south, then had turned in a great loop, to trend north again, leaving a huge tongue of tip-tilted land topped by the imposing Sunup Plateau, cut into a fringed edging by vast and almost impenetrable canyons that were havens of darkness and loneliness.

To the north was the Shivwits Plateau, two or three times larger than the Sanup Plateau, and further north and a great deal easterly, was Fredonia, a good ninety to one hundred miles across the empty country of the Arizona Strip. The last place where Charles Hunter had appeared, if it *had* been him. As Jerry walked through the shadowy darkness of the canyon his heart seemed to waver within him. It was such a vast and comparatively unknown country, almost an isolated world in itself, and trying to find one man in that country seemed almost an impossibility.

The boys did not talk as they slogged on up the canyon. It wasn't quite the place for loose and idle chatter. The walls of the canyon closed in where massive landfalls had dropped from both sides, leaving a narrow, twisted trail down the middle that took time and patience to get through. Sweat ran down Jerry's sides despite the coolness of the wind. Beyond the narrow area, the canyon gradually widened again. Jerry's left boot crushed something and he looked down to see a rusted tin can. It had always been a wonder to him how tin cans could be found in the most isolated and almost impenetrable places, sure sign of civilized man.

Jerry stopped for a breather and the three boys sat down on a rock, eyeing the towering walls, carved in grotesque formations by wind and weather. These battlements and crenelated parapets looked like the remains of some forgotten stronghold of ancient times, a wide and silent world, with a brooding air of mystery about it that chilled the boys more than did the whispering night wind.

Jerry scanned the rim rock high above them. The

fantastic was the ordinary in that huge trough in the ground. To the right the canyon continued, losing itself in the distance, as it appeared to do at the very mouth of the canyon.

"How far?" said Whitey in a very small voice.

"Where did the ferry from the other side of the river land around here?" asked Buck.

"Quite a bit south of us," said Jerry.

"Then there must have been a road or a trail heading north from the landing place, Jerry."

"Somewhere in here," said Jerry.

"Yeh," said Whitey. "But where?"

"All I'm interested in is Lost Canyon," said Jerry. "Linda said it was across the Colorado from Pierce's Ferry, further upstream, somewhere between the Sanup and Shivwits Plateaus."

"Big help," said Buck. "Man, you could hide hundreds of canyons in this country, and none of them, as far as I know, have signposts pointing the way to them, and naming them by name."

"She said you could reach it from the God's Pocket area."

"Yo ho ho," said Whitey dryly.

"There are Indian ruins in it."

"Can't figure Indians wanting to live in here," said Buck. "So far from anyone. So inaccessible."

"That's why they hid in this kind of country," said Whitey, "to get away from their enemies."

"What a life," said Buck. "Man, I'd rather go out and face 'em and have it out."

Whitey flipped a stone at a big tin can. It struck hollowly. "They were a peaceable sort of people. All they wanted to do was plant their little crops and raise their families in peace and quiet. It was the nomads, the raiders who filled them with terror, always raiding and killing, taking what they either couldn't or wouldn't develop on their own."

"Times haven't changed much, have they?" said Buck.

Jerry eyed the big tin can. It hadn't been in there long enough for the paint on it to have been effaced by time or eaten away by rust. He walked over to it. He could just make out the lettering. It had been a can of potato chips. A chilly feeling came over him, but he threw it off. After all, a can that had held potato chips was no indication that his uncle had been in there. He looked up the canyon. Potato chips were hardly the best type of food in a country noted for its intense heat during the spring and summer months, and also for its lack of water.

"What was in it?" asked Buck.

"Potato chips." Jerry looked back at his two friends.

"It's a cinch the Indians didn't leave it behind," said Whitey.

"We can't build up our hopes on an empty tin can," said Buck.

Jerry nodded. He stood up and began to walk toward the upper end of the canyon. As he drew even with a naked pillar of rock that rose from the left-hand rim of the canyon he had the strangest feeling that someone, or something, was watching him. It was the same feeling he had had when he and his friends had first come to the cove where they found *Explorer*. His sixth sense was warning him, but he had no idea why. In such a countryman is always closer to his more primitive emotions. He can see, hear, and sense things that are usually blunted by living in more civilized areas. It was not a new experience for Jerry Hunter, but this night it seemed more vividly intense.

He glanced up at the rock spire that thrust itself up

like a warning finger, silvered by the bright moonlight, and his heart skipped a beat as he saw a white face peering down at him. Cold sweat ran down his sides and his mouth seemed to dry up in an instant. He glanced back at his two friends. Scat was trotting along, tongue hanging out, bright eyes darting from side to side. He did not seem alarmed about anything.

Jerry stole another glance upward, and sure enough, the face was sharply outlined against a darker patch of rock, and it seemed as though the eyes glittered as they looked down into the canyon at the three boys and the dog far below. He didn't know what to do. He felt like an insect specimen neatly pinned on a white card beneath a microscope. Still, there was no sound from Scat and, with all his faults; one had to admit he was a good watchdog.

Buck and Whitey were talking in low voices. Jerry looked back at them, wondering why they didn't see that malignant face and those glittering eyes peering down at them. He wanted to warn them, but his voice dried in his throat. Once again, he looked up at the face. The moon plainly illuminated it, and it was then that he realized it was not a face at all but a sharp discoloration in the rock, with two pieces of mica, or some shiny rock or mineral, forming the two eyes that caught the moonlight on their bright surfaces. Such arc the fears of man, he thought, brought on by the unknown, with no basis to them except in man's mind itself. It was something he had learned in school, but he had never realized the importance of it.

The canyon widened still further and showed three divisions well separated by towering formations that seemed unscalable. Jerry had a desire to climb up out of the deep troughs and see what the upper country was like, but the footing would be treacherous, more so under the uncertain light of the new moon.

"Which one for a starter?" asked Buck as they halted before the three yawning gaps in the solid rock.

"You can have all three of them," said Whitey.

Jerry shrugged. It would take hours to explore each of the branch canyons. He looked down at Scat. "Turn him loose," he said to Whitey.

Whitey slipped the leash. Scat yelped a little, then started toward the center canyon, hesitated, trended left and headed for the end canyon. In a few minutes he had disappeared from sight, followed by the three boys.

Half of the canyon was shrouded in darkness while the further wall was well lit by the moon. A cool wind whispered down the canyon. They walked on for twenty minutes at least, then Buck came to a halt. "Big deal," he said in disgust. "Look."

It was a box canyon, and they were facing a sheer wall from which hung great shards and fragments of rock, seemingly ready to drop if one raised his voice in a shout and set the sleeping echoes flying about. There was no sign of Scat.

"Scat!" called out Whitey.

"Scat! Scat! Scat!" answered the echoes.

It was quiet again. They strained their ears. It was Jerry who heard the grating sound. He walked toward it to find Scat busily digging beneath a rock slab that was half buried in the ground.

Whitey eyed his pet. "This is how you repay me," he said quietly. He pressed the back of his right hand against his forehead.

"Maybe there's a tunnel under there that leads under that rock wall," said Buck. "I have great faith in Scat, Milburn."

"Let's go back," said Jerry. "Whitey, put your leash on Rin Tin Tin there and bring him along."

A driving impatience came over Jerry. He hurried back to the mouth of the canyon and walked around the towering promontory of rock which separated it from the box canyon. He kept on ahead of his two friends, even though this canyon was thicker in shadows than the first one. It was getting late; he was tired from all the diving he had done that day and the moon wouldn't last forever. He had no desire to walk out of that canyon country back to the boat in thick and haunting darkness.

He found a rusted horseshoe beside a rock. Farther on he found a battered cloth-covered canteen, with the dim letters US still legible on the faded material that covered it. These canyons were dotted with such relics of the unknowns, long forgotten, who had penetrated there years past. They meant nothing.

The moon was fully up when he climbed a loose rock slope and found himself in an area where he could look far across the cut-up country, silent and uncanny in the bright moonlight. Thickly furrowed across the gigantic landscape were the dark troughs of many canyons, holding their own secrets against man. It would take years to penetrate each and every one of them and thoroughly examine it. Once again Jerry's heart seemed to fail within him.

His two friends came up behind him, panting with exertion and wet with sweat. "Bingo!" said Buck. "What now?"

"Lordy," said Whitey. "The place is alive with canyons."

"Maybe we ought' a turn Scat loose again," said Buck darkly. "Maybe he'd lose himself forever in one of them."

"Like my uncle," said Jerry quietly.

"I'm sorry, Jerry," said Buck quickly.

"You didn't mean anything," said Jerry. He sat down on a rock and reached for his canteen. He sipped a little water while he studied the terrain. Anything could be hidden in there. An army could be concealed. Tall buildings could be built on the floors of some of those canyons and never be seen from the level of the tops of the canyons. "Lost Canyon!" he said. He smashed a fist into his other palm.

Buck looked at Whitey and shrugged. "We can go back and try the other one," he said.

"What's the use," said Jerry.

"Well, I'm not giving up."

"Me neither," said Whitey. He was tired and beads of perspiration dewed his face, but the spirit was still in his eyes.

"Whurf," said Scat. He trotted back toward the canyon through which they had just passed.

"Wait a minute," said Buck. He walked forward and climbed a rock ledge. "There's a road or something 'way over there."

They climbed up beside him. Faintly seen against the dun earth were twin ruts, hardly discernible, but certainly manmade. They came from far to the right, looped past a ragged ridge, then trended north to disappear in a deep swale of ground.

"Maybe that's the road from Pierce's Ferry," said Whitey.

"Probably," said Buck. "Looks like it's been there a long time." He looked at Jerry. "Long enough to have been there in the '80s?"

"Probably," said Jerry. "The Mormon party crossed at Pierce's Ferry, started through the Grand Wash area, heading for Saint George. They never got there. Vanished! Men, horses, mules, and gold."

The three of them surveyed the area. Whitey shivered. "They might be right near us," he said.

"Who?" demanded Buck.

"The bones of those men, and maybe the gold as well."

"If it was bandits, they'd have taken the gold."

"It could have been Indians," said Jerry. "Piutes probably. They'd have had no use for gold. In those days anyway."

"We need a mine detector," said Whitey.

"I saw a rusted horseshoe back there," said Jerry. "There was a canteen lying back there too. Marked US. Could have been dropped by a soldier, or someone who just happened to have an army canteen."

"Like a Mormon heading for Saint George with his saddlebags full of gold," said Whitey.

Without another word, the three of them started back through the canyon to where they had found the relics. They could tell them nothing. Perhaps they had been dropped in recent times. They walked slowly back to the mouth of the canyon and stopped to look toward the third of the canyons, now covered in shadows, for the moon was racing through the night sky toward the west.

"Have we got time to start exploring that one?" said Buck.

"The moon won't last much longer," said Whitey.

"I vote we give it a try anyway," said Buck. "I don't mind walking back to the boat in darkness."

Almost as an echo to his brave words came a haunting cry from high on the rimrock above them. Like the call of a soul from another world. Then it died away.

The boys stood stock still.

"Coyote?" said Whitey.

"Mountain lion?" said Buck.

"Look at Scat," said Jerry quietly.

The little mutt was staring up at the rimrock, lips drawn back from his sharp white teeth, eyes wide in his head, every muscle rigid, tail straight and stiff as a ramrod, and not a sound came from him.

Once again, the cry arose, drifting on the quiet night, with an eerie, uncanny quality about it, and each of those three boys knew in his own heart that it was not a coyote, or a mountain lion, or anything else that was alive, animal *or* human.

The silent command came. The three of them moved swiftly down the central canyon, back toward the distant and unseen Colorado, their stumbling feet winged by fear.

Chapter 12

The Search for Lost Canyon

FEAR DRIFTED OVER THE CANYON ON SILENT velvety wings and cast its miasma over the three explorers as they passed the grotesque rock formation which had frightened Jerry earlier. He did not look at it as they came closer to it, not wanting to see that face, even though he knew he should not be afraid.

He looked back along the wide and silent canyon, dropping behind Buck and Whitey as they forged on, breathing hard. That weird cry in the night was enough to unsettle anyone's nerves. He was fifty feet behind the others when at last he stopped looking backward and turned to catch up with them. It was then that he saw the face again. He grinned weakly, shaking a fist up at it as it watched him with those unmoving eyes. "Won't scare me this time," he said under his breath. He looked away from it and then a cold feeling swept over him, and a ball of ice seemed to form in his stomach. The face was not in the same place where he had seen it before. He looked ahead and realized he had mistaken the nearby rock formation for that which actually had the face marked upon it. The real rock formation was a good one hundred yards down the canyon.

He screwed his courage to the breaking point and looked up at the face that was closest to him. The moon was drifting behind a cloud layer and, the instant before it withdrew its light from the canyon wall, Jerry distinctly saw the moist glittering eyes, burning from the lean pointed face, and the mouth opened wide like that of a Greek tragedy mask. Then the face vanished in the darkness of the shadows like a mask worked by a black clothed hand unseen against a black background.

He was sprinting fifty yards from the rock formation when the thin, eerie sound drifted from the rimrock and died away in a haunting echo.

Jerry was still behind the others when the moon passed further west, plunging the canyon behind them into full darkness, although there was yet enough light ahead of them to see their way through the area where the fantastic rock formations looked like nature's imitation of medieval Carcassonne or Mont-Saint-Michel in France.

The wind was colder now but it did nothing to alleviate the perspiration that dripped down Jerry's body as he chased after the others. It seemed to him that the thorny vegetation thrust out wiry, clutching hands to tear at his clothing and flesh. His lungs seemed to be on fire when at last they reached the last stretch of the canyon leading down to the cove. The moon was still sinning down from across the Colorado, lighting the cove and the last hundred yards or so of the canyon.

Their pounding feet echoed faintly from the canyon walls. Jerry saw the water shimmering with reflected light. Suddenly Whitey, who was well in the lead, stopped, thrust up a warning hand and darted behind a boulder followed by Scat. Buck plunged in behind him. Jerry took cover behind a shoulder of rock and peered down toward the water to see what had alarmed Whitey. There was nothing to see.

He wiped the sweat from his face and tried to ease his harsh breathing. He was sure it could easily be heard at least a quarter of a mile away. Jerry looked at Whitey. Whitey held up a warning hand, then pointed down toward the cove.

The moonlight reflected from something white as it moved slowly into the cove. Jerry's heart skipped a beat. It was about a twenty-two-footer, twin-engine, with a small cabin forward, and a canvas top folded down behind the windshield. He had seen that boat before, or one just like it, although it wasn't an uncommon type. The last time he had noted one like it had been the day he and his two friends had taken the three girls out on Lake Mead. He had the downright uneasy feeling that this was the same boat.

A big man stepped up out of the cockpit and walked forward alongside the low cabin to the foredeck. He got down on his knees to look at the water, as though he were looking for obstacles. Another man was at the wheel. A third man came out of the cabin and leaned over the side. He had a big nose and a trim mustache and as Jerry watched him, he took cigarette makings from his shirt pocket and deftly fashioned a smoke. He lighted it and as he did so the flare of the match revealed his face. There wasn't any doubt in Jerry's mind now. It was the same man who had poked about *Huntress* the first time the boys had taken her out. The camouflaged fisherman in the fair-weather boat. The man who had probably tailed them to Temple Bar Landing, for they had seen his boat beached there. The man who had been prowling about the Hunter house in Boulder City. How had Andrew Tyson described Webb Macklin? "Good-sized man. Rather large nose. Trim mustache."

The only sound in the cove was the soft throbbing of one of the big outboard motors of the boat. It echoed back and forth from the canyon walls. Wavelets tinkled on the rocky shore from the wash of the boat as it turned and cruised toward the far side of the cove, out of sight of the three watchers in the canyon.

Jerry darted forward and crowded in beside his two friends. "Well," he said dryly, "we were wondering where they were."

"If they come up here," said Buck, "we'll be trapped behind this boulder."

"Follow me," said Jerry. He ran softly to the far side of the canyon and took cover in a tangle of shattered rock that had fallen from the overhanging wall above. His two friends followed him. Just as they took cover, the boat appeared again. It moved slowly until it was within twenty feet of the ledge beneath which *Huntress* was hidden.

"Oh, man!" said Whitey. He looked down at Scat. "Don't you dare make a sound."

"See anything, Siskin?" called out the mustached man to the man on the foredeck.

"Not a thing, Mac," answered the big man. "Where'd them blasted kids get to?"

"They're around here somewhere," said Webb Macklin. "Move us over to that rock ledge there, Carl."

The boat was maneuvered until it bumped gently against the rock ledge, and it could not have been more than five feet from *Huntress*. The man named Siskin stepped out on the ledge and made a bow line fast to a projecting spike of rock. He looked up the canyon. "Looks like a box canyon, Mae," he said.

"Maybe. The canyon we're looking for is within half a mile of here. Somewhere up there is Lost Canyon."

"If it exists," said the man at the wheel.

"It does, blast you!" snapped Macklin. "Andy Tyson said it exists. Jim Bedloe said it exists."

"Yeh! Yeh! So what?"

Macklin stepped out on the ledge. "Maybe you'll believe it when I tell you that Chuck Hunter once told me he had been in it, not more than a few miles from God's Pocket."

There was no answer from Carl.

"That shut you up, eh, Carl?" said Macklin. "I wish I had stayed friendly with Hunter in those days. I might have learned more. Not me! I had to pull a fast one on him and he never had any use for me since then. Then he had to vanish in here somewhere."

Their voices came clearly to the boys through some fluke of acoustics.

"We were so close behind him when he disappeared," said Macklin. "Beats me how he vanished like that, boat and all. Remember, Siskin?"

The big man nodded. "You still think them slippery kids know where that Mormon gold is hidden?"

"Not exactly," said Macklin. He looked up the darkening canyon. "But I think they know more than we do."

"That ain't hard," said Carl.

Macklin turned slowly. "Shut up!" he snapped. "We know those punks are in here somewhere, and they ain't picking dewberries. Once we spot that boat, we can get a hue on where they are operating. After that, we know what to do, eh, Siskin?"

The big man grinned. "How much gold did you say was in the deal?"

"About a hundred thousand from all I've heard."

Their boat drifted out from the rock ledge, leaving a three-foot gap. It was then that Whitey gripped Jerry's arm and pointed down toward the boat. From where they were they could see the mud-plastered white side of *Huntress* beneath the ledge. She had evidently been attracted by the suction of the bigger boat. If she drifted out into the open...

Macklin and Siskin walked to the end of the ledge closest to the shore while Carl stayed in the boat, staring up the dark trough of the canyon. Neither of the two men on the ledge could see *Huntress* unless she drifted out into the open, but if Carl happened to look to his right, and downward, he'd hardly miss seeing her.

Huntress drifted a little more. Another foot and she'd show beneath the edge of the ledge.

"It's too dark to go poking up there, Mac," said Siskin. "Maybe we ought' a moor here tonight and start out in the morning?"

"That's all we need," hissed Whitey to Jerry.

Fate works in peculiar ways. Out of the silence of the upper canyon drifted the eerie keening cry like that of a lost soul. It was enough to chill even the stoutest heart. The moon was suddenly gone and darkness filled the canyon and the cove.

"What was *that?*" asked Carl.

"Mountain Hon," said Siskin.

"I never heard no mountain lion sound like *that!*"

There were a few minutes of silence, and then the cry came again, closer this time, echoing through the darkness.

"Pull the boat in, Siskin," said Webb Macklin. "I ain't

figuring on getting a good night's sleep with that thing crying up there like a lost soul. We can come back in the morning."

The boat bumped against the ledge. The two men stepped in. One of the motors throbbed softly. The boat moved slowly out of the cove and the sound of its motor died away on the Colorado.

"That was too close for comfort," said Buck.

"Comfort, he says," said Whitey. He looked up the canyon. "With *that* prowling around?"

They walked down toward the boat. "Maybe we ought to camp on shore tonight," said Buck. "We can keep the boat hidden and leave before dawn."

There was no answer until they reached the ledge, then Scat turned slowly, teeth bared, lips drawn tightly back, eyes staring up the dark canyon. A low growl came from deep in his throat.

"We can sleep in the boat and still leave before dawn," said Whitey. "You won't get Mrs. Cramer's favorite son Milburn to sleep on *that* shore tonight."

"Amen," said Jerry.

They eased the boat out and while Whitey prepared sandwiches from cold meat. Buck walked out to the mouth of the cove where he could see the river and still signal back to the boat with his flashlight. They took turns standing guard until all of them had eaten, then they prepared their packs for the trip the next day into the canyon country.

They crouched low in the boat and pulled it far under the ledge. Jerry could reach up and touch the cool, damp surface of the rock overhead. They bunked down, depending on Scat to alert them if anyone appeared.

Thick darkness shrouded the Colorado country. The water lapped against the shores, and the soft murmur of the rushing river came to the boys, mingled with the rustling of the brush.

Jerry was dead beat from his diving that day, as well as from the tough and rugged hike up the canyon. He dropped off to sleep.

Sometime during the night, he opened his eyes. He lay very still, listening to the soft breathing of his friends. The night sounds were the same the murmur of the great river, the waves lapping the shore, the rustling of the brush. Then he heard something else. A grating noise and it seemed to come from directly overhead, as though something were moving atop the ledge. He raised his head and peered from the boat but could see nothing except the dark surface of the water. He sat there a long time, then dropped back on his blankets. He was almost asleep when he heard the grating sound again. Cold sweat greased his body as he sat up again.

Fifteen minutes went past, and Jerry heard nothing but the sounds of the night. Sleep was too strong for him and he dropped off.

The wind shifted up the canyon. The three sleepers in the boat did not hear anything, and perhaps no one else did either, but sometimes, when the wind blew strongly from the upper canyon, it seemed to carry an eerie crying sound, hardly distinguishable above the noise of the wind.

They were up long before the first light of dawn. Whitey and Buck carried the gear up on the shore while Buck slipped back into the water, towing cut brush with him to hang along the sides of the boat after he had pushed it as far back beneath the ledge as he could and moored it fast. He swam easily back to shore in the darkness, dressed quickly, then joined his two friends.

The first pewter traces of light showed in the eastern

sky as they breasted the cold and searching wind that swept down the darkly shadowed canyon.

Dawn light was filtering down into the canyon when they reached the peculiar rock formations. They were making good time, and the lighter it got, the better they felt. It would be a long hot day in those great furrows of rock, but it was better to have the heat than the cold of darkness, and the unknown things that concealed themselves within it.

They took a breather where the three canyons met.

Whitey reached behind himself for his canteen and his questing hand touched nothing. "Blast!" he said. "My canteen is gone!"

"You leave it in the boat?" said Buck. "I'll run all the way back and get it for you, Milburn."

Whitey shook his head. An odd look was on his face.

Jerry looked quickly at him. "Where did you leave it?" he asked sharply.

Whitey opened his mouth and then closed it.

"Well?" asked Buck coldly.

Whitey swallowed hard. "I was putting on my pack and my canteen was in the way. I unhooked the canteen and put it down on a rock."

"Right on the shore, eh, Milburn? In plain view of anyone who just might happen to come into the cove?" said Buck.

Whitey smiled weakly. "Heh, heh, heh..."

Jerry stood up and looked down the canyon. "That's a sure enough signpost," he said. "The only thing they don't know is which canyon will go up. At first anyway. Come on!" He led the way swiftly toward the third of the canyons. There was no use getting angry with Whitey. Anyone of the three of them could have done it. "Walk on rock!" he said.

They looked back as they entered the mouth of the canyon. The canyon beyond it was well lit, but there was no sign of life. They had left no tracks indicating they had entered this particular canyon. Jerry turned and led the way into the cool, shadowy darkness of the canyon, as yet unlighted by the rising sun.

Chapter 13

The Haunted Water Hole

THE CANYON HAD BEEN ERODED LIKE BEADS ON a string, the wide parts being the beads, while the narrow parts were the strings between each bead. There were many of them, and at times the narrow parts were choked with fallen rock, earth, and the clutching brush that ripped at clothing and flesh like fishhooks, reluctant to let anything pass by without a protest. Shadowy as it was, the canyon began to fill slowly with the day's heat, and the exertion of forcing a way through the opposing passages drew perspiration from every pore.

It was a good thing that there was but one way in and conversely, one way out, for if there had been a number of entrance ways, some of them blind alleys, a man could get lost in such a place and spend days trying to find his way out, if he ever *did* find his way out.

The eerie feeling came over Jerry Hunter that he and his two companions had somehow wandered from the face of the known earth onto some far distant planet, as yet unexplored. Now and then he would look at the high walls of the twisted canyon to see the slice of blue sky, unflecked by clouds, and he felt much like a prisoner does who sees a patch of blue sky through the barred window of his cell.

"Indian ruins," said Whitey suddenly.

"Where?" demanded Jerry. His head snapped up.

"I was just commenting," said Whitey dryly. "Even an Indian would hardly build anything in here."

By high noon Jerry knew they'd never be able to make it back to the boat that day. The heat was thickening in the canyon and their water supply was short by a third. There were no signs of water in the canyon.

In the early afternoon they had reached the end of the trail. The canyon ended in a naked towering wall of salmon and pink hued rock with huge masses of tumbled rock at the base of it. Three pairs of eyes scanned the walls on each side. There was no possible way for the canyon to continue.

"End of the line," said Whitey despondently.

Buck looked back over his shoulder. "We can hardly make it back to the boat now," he said. "We'd be more than lucky if we reached the main canyon before dark."

Jerry nodded. He felt sick deep within himself. He had been almost sure they were on the right track, but now the canyon had proved to be a box, and there were no signs of ruins in it. He looked up at the nearest wall.

"I know what you're thinking," said Buck. "I'll try it."

"The rock looks pretty crumbly," said Whitey.

Buck took his coiled line of nylon rope. "I'll give it a try," he said quietly. He peeled off his belt and pack, took Jerry's field glasses, and began to climb the talus slope until he could reach the base of the almost sheer wall. He formed a noose, hurled it upward with an underhand swing and looped it neatly about a projecting rock. It took a matter of minutes for him to pull himself up to the rock and then begin to pick hand holds until he was a quarter of the way up the wall. Whitey turned to look the other way. Jerry wet his dry lips. If Buck fell and was seriously injured, they'd never be able to get him out of there.

Halfway up the wall Buck stopped to sit on a ledge with his legs dangling over the edge. He cupped his hands about his mouth. "No use," he called down. "Can't get any higher."

"No use...no use...no use..." echoed the canyon. "Can't get any higher...can't get any higher...can't get any higher..."

"Great," said Whitey.

"Look around the canyon," called Jerry. "Maybe you can spot something."

Buck swept the canyon with the field glasses, then looked down at Jerry. "No go," he said.

Whitey and Jerry sat down to wait for Buck, eating their belated lunch as they did so. "Sure makes a man thirsty," said Whitey.

"We'll have to go easy on the water," said Jerry. "There's only two canteens between the three of us, and mine is half empty."

Buck walked slowly down the slope, wiping the sweat from his face. He picked up his canteen, then looked quickly at Jerry. "Did you empty this one first?" he asked.

"Haven't touched it yet," said Jerry. "We'll use my water first."

"First, last and always," said Buck. "This one is empty." He looked down at the place where it had been lying. A dark wet patch showed on the dry rock. "The cap must have been loose when I dropped it here."

Jerry hefted his canteen. "Unless we find water," he

said quietly, "this will have to do us until we get back to the river."

"Some time tomorrow," said Buck.

They all looked at each other. Jerry stood up. "The first thing we better do is find water," he said. "Forget everything else."

The sun was slanting far to the west when at last they gave up. There wasn't a drop of water to be found anywhere.

"Looks like we better head out of here before dawn," said Buck. "The cooler it is, the better time we can make. It's going to be a dry run all the way, men."

Jerry looked up at the rimrock. A hawk hung in the air above the canyon, floating near the end wall, looking for prey with its telescopic eyes. Suddenly, for no apparent reason, it veered sharply and shot off down the wind, flying swiftly. Jerry idly wondered what had frightened it.

The knowledge that water was in short supply made their thirst even greater. A pebble held beneath the tongue did little good. There had been no rain in that country for many months, so there was hardly a chance of finding a hollow filled with rainwater.

There was deep despair in Jerry as the sun finally withdrew itself beyond the distant mountains and the shadows formed in the deep canyon. Another day was almost gone. The next day would be spent getting back to the boat. Another day to look for yet another canyon.

"Where's Scat?" said Whitey suddenly.

The little dog had spent most of the afternoon lying beneath a rock ledge, seeking what little coolness there was in that heat-soaked canyon. Now he was gone.

"Maybe he's smarter than we are at that," said Buck. "Maybe he pulled foot for the Colorado."

"Not Scat," said Whitey. "He'd never leave me." He whistled sharply again and again, hearing nothing but the echoes and the dry whispering of the wind.

They looked about the canyon but there was no trace of the dog. When the last light was fading away, Scat appeared from the far end of the canyon, trotting briskly along, tail flying in the air. Whitey gripped him about the neck. "Say," he said sharply, "his muzzle is wet!"

"Tell him to go back," said Jerry.

Scat barked as Whitey told him to go back to the water. He trotted off at a steady pace, with the three boys right behind him, heedless of thorny brush and sharp-edged rocks. They saw Scat vanish around a huge rock shoulder and, when they followed him, he was nowhere to be seen.

The darkness was thickening. Suddenly it was unutterably lonely, and the wind began to whisper in strange voices through the tangled brush.

"Scat!" called Whitey.

No answer.

"Scat!" called Ruck.

No answer.

"Beats me," said Whitey.

Jerry saw a movement in a tangle of brush and shattered rock at the foot of a sheer wall. His heart skipped a beat until he saw that it was Scat, with an expression on his face as though to say: "What's all the fuss about?"

This time Whitey was right behind the mutt as Scat vanished again. Buck and Jerry followed him. There, almost hidden by the thick veil of brush, was an opening in the seemingly solid rock face through which a cool draft flowed. The two boys worked their way into it, with just about elbow room on each side of them, until they heard Scat barking up ahead.

Fifty yards more of dark passageway and then it lightened ahead. Water splashed. Whitey was singing softly. Jerry and Ruck came out into a large circular area, like a huge hole bored down from the upper area high above them, floored with white sand and rounded boulders. Off to the right, beneath an overhanging wall of rock, was a pool about fifteen feet wide, formed in the rock, with a thin, silvery-looking trickle of water flowing down the inside wall from some unseen source. The overflow of water tinkled through a narrow trough in the rock and vanished into the wall on the far side of the circular area.

Whitey was lapping up the water like a dog. He grinned back over his shoulder. "Maybe we ought'a let Scat take over the running of tins expedition," he said with a grin.

"Is it real?" asked Buck.

Whitey scooped up a double handful and flung it at Buck's heated face. Buck closed his eyes and licked the water as it ran down his face. "I don't believe it," he said ecstatically.

It was real, all right, Jerry found when he dropped belly flat and thrust his burning face into the water. It was pure, clear, sweet, and *cold*. He sat up and wiped the water from his face. "Beats me," he said quietly, "but I'm not the one to question a miracle."

Buck leaned back against a rock. "This is the place," he said in satisfaction. "We can make this our camp tonight. Too bad we have to leave it to look for Lost Canyon."

Jerry said nothing. The thought was in his mind too. Even the thought of finding water could hardly erase the fact from his mind that they had failed in their mission.

"Well, anyway, our boys didn't find us today," said Whitey.

Buck looked up at the irregularly shaped patch of dark sky. "About the only way they could find us now would be to look down into here."

"Just the same," said Jerry, "we'd better not light a fire. They could smell it, even if they couldn't see it there will be a moon later on. Well make our camp under the rock overhang beside the pool, so that no one can see us from above. Scat will warn us if anyone comes into the passageway."

When the thick darkness came and filled the great hole like ink, Jerry wasn't quite so sure of himself. The night has a voice and an entity of its own, quite different from that of the day, and man has not yet managed to overcome the difference in his innermost feelings between the darkness and the light.

It was very quiet in the canyon. There was a faint tinkling of water in the pool. There was no wind. High above that great hole in the solid rock was the dark blue patch of the sky, stippled with ice chip stars, clear and sharp against the blue. Tired as they were, none of the boys could sleep. There was absolutely nothing to do but sit there in the darkness, hardly visible to each other, waiting for the rising of the moon to fill the hole with cold, silvery light.

Jerry occupied himself by looking up at the top of the hole, waiting for the first faint tinge of light. Suddenly it came, and the light spilled into the hole. As the moon kept rising, the silver light crept down the wall, reached the bottom, then moved slowly, almost imperceptibly across to the pool and, the first thing one knew, the moonlight was glinting from the tiny wavelets.

Jerry rolled over and looked down into the pool. It was only a few feet deep, and he could see every pebble, ripple, and mark on the sandy bottom. He thrust his hand into the water and could see every line on it. He could hardly remember ever having seen such clear water in all his years in this country.

"Like crystal," said Whitey.

"I would have been satisfied with an old buffalo wallow full of rainwater," said Buck. "This was hard to believe."

"What's next on the agenda?" asked Whitey.

Courage and voices had returned with the coming of the moonlight, and as long as it held sway, short as it would be in the deep hole, their spirits would rise and stay high.

Jerry leaned back against a boulder and traced his fingers through the sand. There were many unexplained things that had been plaguing him. The strange and eerie crying in the night. The site of Lost Canyon. The finding of the *Explorer,*

The moon was fully on the pool now. Jerry looked at Buck. "I think we can try the upper country for a while tomorrow," he said. "Maybe we can look *down* into Lost Canyon, rather than try to find it from the bottom, so to speak." He looked at the pool again. Something caught his attention—something that was spreading slowly across the pool from the side next to the rock wall. He narrowed his eyes and glanced at the others. Whitey was lying on his back, staring up at the moonlit sky with a smile on his face. Buck was examining the sole of one of his boots. Jerry tried another look at the pool. The stain was wider, almost to the middle of the pool now. His stomach moiled. The stain was red. As *red as freshly spilled blood...*

"Jerry?" said Buck.

Jerry's eyes were wide in his head. His throat went dry.

"Jerry?" said Buck.

Jerry pointed at the pool. The red stain was three-quarters of the way across now, sending out wavering tendrils toward the edge of the pool. Under the light of the moon, the pool was rapidly becoming blood red in color.

"What the!" said Buck. His eyes bugged out.

Whitey raised himself on an elbow just as the pool became solidly red like the overflow basin in an abattoir. His jaw dropped as he stared at the pool. Then he pulled back his feet and moved away from the pool.

Already the moon was withdrawing its light from the hole, but there was still enough of it to show the red hue of the pool.

"What is it? What's happened?" said Buck in a strangled voice.

Jerry got to his feet, and like Whitey, he withdrew from the once pleasant brink of the pool, now a thing of horror. It was too much for his nerves. Panic began to jibber in the back of his mind and fear fought for control of his waning courage.

It was deathly quiet except for the faint tinkling of the water in the pool. The overflow was red now for the full width of the bottom of the great hole, like a stripe of red ribbon against the whiteness of a starched shirt bosom.

"This place is haunted," said Whitey in a low, dry voice.

"Cut it out!" snapped Jerry.

"How else can you explain *that*?"

Jerry cut a hand sideways. The light was beginning to fail. "There's an explanation! I'm sure of it!"

Scat got to his feet. He stared up at the opening, high above them, teeth bared, and eyes set and unblinking.

The cry came softly at first, hardly audible, then it rose swiftly until it seemed to fill the hole and the sheer loneliness and eeriness of it raised the hairs on the backs of the boys' necks.

There was no place to run this time. They'd have to stand and take it, beside that blood red pool, in the cold, gathering darkness, with that eldritch crying drifting through the night to turn bones into marrow and warm blood into red ice crystals.

The crying died away, and the silence that followed seemed even worse, with the haunting fear that mingled with it.

Jerry leaned against the rock wall, sick to his soul. Only his faith kept him from screaming aloud in panic or bolting from that place of terror. Gradually he got control, until before all the light was gone; he kneeled beside the pool and filled a cup with the water.

"You ain't going to drink *that*, are you?" said Whitey weakly.

Jerry ignored him. He dipped a finger into the water and saw that it hardly stained the finger. He gathered his courage and then sipped the water. There was a slightly different taste to it. He could not identify it, but it didn't have the salty taste of blood, and for that he was more than thankful.

Buck looked at Jerry. "Well?" he said.

Jerry shrugged. "Doesn't taste like blood to me."

"There's a lot of water in there to dilute it," said Whitey.

Jerry pulled off his boots and socks, rolled up his Levis, then waded into the pool, feeling his way far back until he was against the rock wall, dark with the thin film of water that flowed into the pool from some unknown source deep within the living rock. He passed his hand over the water, rubbing it against the rock surface, then lit a match. For a moment he felt a little sick and uneasy, for his palm was smeared bloody red. He sniffed at it, then tasted it, and the taste was flat and earthy, not like blood at all. He moved along the rock wall and saw something rounded on a natural shelf. He lit another match and saw a clay pot, of black-and-white design, with stylized figures of animals painted on the baked clay. He explored the niche with his free hand and felt broken shards of pottery and withdrew an ancient sandal of husking. "You can tell Lost Canyon by the Indian ruins that are in it," he said aloud. The match flickered out. He walked back to the edge of the pool. "Give me a flashlight, Whitey."

He walked back under the overhang and flicked the powerful light of the torch upward. An irregularly shaped hole revealed itself, and alongside the rock wall, dug into the flat surface, were foot and hand holds leading up into the hole. A draft of cold air played about his face. He pulled himself up to the first footholds, then stood up to pull himself up higher until his head and shoulders were within the hole. He was about to flick on the torch again when he happened to look up. High above him, barely discernible, was a small oval patch of the night sky, dotted with a few winking stars. He lit the torch and saw that there were other feet and hand holds above him. He raised the torch. The strong light picked out the shape of a ladder, crudely formed of saplings, bound together with rawhide or withes, thrusting itself up the rough-sided tube in the living rock. Beyond the first ladder was another, resting on a ledge, and above that yet another.

Jerry reached the first ladder and tested it. It was a little shaky. He examined the lashings, and a queer feeling came over him. Old as the ladder evidently was, *the lashings were comparatively new, and well made.* It wasn't only the cold draft of air that made him shiver. He let himself down into the pool, then waded ashore.

"Well?" said Whitey.

Jerry told them of what he had found.

"Maybe it's Lost Canyon up there," said Buck. "The pottery and the ladders were made by Indians."

"Yeh," said Whitey thoughtfully, "but who made the new lashings?"

"There's one way to find out," said Jerry. "There will likely be plenty of moonlight still up there. Are you both game to go up?"

"That's why we came," said Buck.

Whitey nodded. "Let's get what we need and cache the rest."

"Rope, flashlights, water, the axe, and Scat, of course," said Jerry.

They worked swiftly and cached what they did not need under the overhanging rock wall. In a few minutes the three of them were standing at the foot of the first ladder. Jerry tested it with his foot, then began to climb, carrying linked coils of nylon rope over his shoulder. He did not hesitate, climbing swiftly and steadily, until he reached the top and pulled himself out on naked rock beneath a sheer cliff. The opening was walled in by thick and thorny shrub. He looked over a low shrub and saw that the narrow and twisted canyon beyond the scrub was well lighted by the moon. It was early yet, and there would be some hours of moonlight yet in the canyon.

He lowered the rope and minutes later hauled Scat up. Buck and Whitey came up the ladder one at a time, using the rope as a handhold in case a rung broke. Buck whistled softly as he saw the narrow canyon, dreaming in the clear, cold light.

"Curiouser and curiouser," said Whitey. "I'm beginning to feel like Alice in Wonderland."

Jerry pushed his way through the brush. Moonlight sparkled on a pool close to the rock wall, quite similar to the one far below them. At the far edge the water trickled into a narrow crack in the rock, to vanish from sight. Jerry knew that it must emerge again, far below, to form the pool they had just left.

He knelt by the side of the pool. Scattered on the hard earth was a reddish substance. He picked some of it up and sniffed at it. It was earth of some kind, almost blood red in color. He scooped up a handful and dropped it in the pool. In a matter of minutes, the water had been dyed blood red and was flowing over the lip of the crack. He looked back at Buck and Whitey. "There's the answer to *that*," he said.

"Easy, wasn't it?" said Whitey cheerfully.

Buck turned and looked up the dreamlike canyon. "Yeh," he said quietly, "but who put the earth into the pool?"

As they walked toward the first great rock shoulder of the canyon the thought that Buck had uttered filled their minds to the exclusion of everything else.

Chapter 14

Ruins in the Moonlight

THEY ROUNDED THE FIRST HUGE SHOULDER OF rock, carefully picking their way over the rough ground. Whitey was in the lead. He stopped suddenly, staring up at something on the towering eastern wall of the canyon. Buck looked up as well, and his jaw dropped. When Jerry's turn came, his jaw dropped too.

The arched roof of an enormous cave extended for many yards along the canyon wall, and filling it was a dead and silent city of stone and mortar, deathly white under the rays of the moon. Several terraces had been formed on the slope beneath the huge and arching roof of the cave. Windows and doors stood out in dark and sharp relief against the pale, whitish rock of the ancient structures. Here and there, a rounded tower thrust up its broken head, breaking the irregular line of the lower structures. It looked like a brooding castle of medieval times, transported by black magic to this lost canyon in one of the loneliest and most isolated parts of Arizona.

Nothing moved in the windless air. Beneath the lowest terrace was a long talus slope, stippled with dark brush. The terrace was bordered with a low wall of loose, un-mortared stones. There was no sign of life under the uncanny light of the moon.

Jerry broke the spell. "Come on," he said. He walked toward the talus slope with the others crowding his back.

They slogged up the slope until they reached the wall, and it was as though an invisible wall held them back as well as the material one in front of them. They saw a wide terrace of flat and irregularly shaped stones, with the interstices between them filled with hard packed earth as smooth as concrete. Here and there the mouths of openings showed on the pavement, with crude ladders protruding from the unknown depths. The buildings were pierced with very small rudely shaped windows and T shaped doors. Ladders rested against the higher walls around the space. Sagging wooden walkways, supported by beams thrust from the walls, formed the means of entry into second and third-floor dwellings.

Close up, the structures showed signs of ruin. Roofs had collapsed, filling interiors; walls had crumbled, littering pavements and passageways; clumps of brush had sprung up in shallow earth pockets. In scattered spots, a warped scrub tree fought for life in the shallow earth.

"How long do you think they've been here?" asked Buck.

"Hundreds of years," said Jerry quietly.

"I think we've come to the right place," said Whitey.

Jerry looked up and down the narrow canyon. He could see why this canyon was known as Lost Canyon, for it could hardly be seen if a person were too far away from either rim while, even from the air, it would be almost impossible to see the silent ruins well hidden under the great overhanging roof formed by the cliff.

Perhaps the ruins were known to exist; that wasn't unusual. There are many such ruins, large and small, scattered throughout the southwest, in almost inaccessible places, hardly worth the effort for one to visit them; and at certain times of the year the trails would be impassable. Only the better-known ruins, easily reached by road, were visited by the tourist public, leaving the majority of them to be viewed by the lone wanderer or those hardy enough to penetrate into the wilderness that protected them from view.

"What do we do now?" said Buck.

Jerry stepped over the wall. "Keep looking," he said.

"Maybe we ought to stay together," suggested Whitey quickly. "For safety you know. Ha, ha, ha…

"Ha, ha, ha," repeated Buck.

The echoes drifted back from the overhanging wall. "Ha…ha…ha…ha…ha…ha…"

Jerry walked past one of the ladders that protruded from the hole in the floor of the terrace, recognizing it as the entrance to a kiva, the underground meeting place of one of the men's societies of the cliff dwellers who had left there so long ago. He walked between two of the larger structures until he found himself at the rear of the row of buildings, where the rock wall behind the dwellings formed a rough, triangularly shaped corridor that ran the full length of the entire formation of buildings. It was dark, and it echoed hollowly.

Jerry peered both ways. He flicked on his flashlight and walked to the right, probing into the darkness with the strong light of the hand torch. He rounded the jutting corner of a building and stopped short, while the hair rose on the back of his neck and fear ran through his mind.

"What is it?" asked Buck.

Jerry wordlessly stepped aside. The pool of light from the torch revealed a skeleton, partially wrapped in decayed rags, lying on its back, sightless eyes staring up at the rock roof overhead, bony hands clasping something that protruded from the hollow rib cage. It was an arrow, with the dusty feathers still fletched to the shaft. A dusty hat lay to one side and a canteen was beside it.

"White man?" said Whitey in a very tiny voice.

Jerry nodded. "I think so."

"Killed by the cliff dwellers?" said Buck.

Jerry shook his head. "These cliff dwellers left here hundreds of years before any white man penetrated this country."

"Then who killed him?" said Buck.

Jerry flicked the light about. A rusted and dusty rifle lay on the far side of the skeleton. "Likely he was wounded elsewhere and crawled in here to die," he said. "He was probably ambushed by more modern Indians than the cliff dwellers. Piutes probably. They wouldn't have followed him in here. Too superstitious. They usually avoided these places. Maybe he knew that. A lot of good it did him."

"He's been here a long time," said Buck.

"Maybe seventy-five or eighty years?" said Whitey.

"Sure," said Jerry. "Why?"

"About the time those Mormons crossed the Colorado at Pierce's Ferry with a hundred thousand dollars' worth of gold bullion in their mule kyacks?"

"There were eight or nine of them," said Jerry. "Also eight or nine horses, maybe four or five mules. You see any traces of them around here, Sherlock?"

Whitey shook his head. "You said yourself he might have crawled in here to die. Where did he crawl from?"

"The canyon," said Buck. "I vote we take a look down there."

It wasn't hard to leave that place of brooding death. There was still plenty of moonlight in the quiet canyon. The floor of it was a tangled jungle of detritus, talus, shin tangle and wait a bit bush.

Far to one side, beneath an overhanging rock, out of sight of the ruins, the moon shone coldly on yet another gruesome relic of the past, a headless skeleton, with other bones missing, probably hauled away by scavenging animals. This one had no clothing about him.

In twenty minutes, they found three more skeletons, piled together in a circular shelter of rocks. Two of them had bullet holes in their skulls, while the third literally bristled with arrow shafts. None of them had a scrap of clothing about them.

"Well?" said Buck as they walked slowly up the canyon.

Jerry looked up at the high, serrated walls of the deep and narrow trough. "I figure it this way. They might, or might not have been our missing Mormons, but they were white men. They were ambushed somewhere around here. Three of them made it into that rock circle to fight it out to the last. One of them made it up to the dwellings. Another either died on the way or lay there until the Piutes caught up with him. You noticed the only one still clothed was the one up behind the dwellings. The others had been killed and stripped of weapons and clothing. We haven't found any mule or horse skeletons. The Piutes wouldn't kill valuable animals. I'm willing to bet the rest of the human skeletons are lying somewhere in this canyon."

"Maybe they escaped?"

Jerry shook his head. "Not likely. According to

Andrew Tyson, those men were trusted members of the Mormon Church. If any of them had survived, the records of the church would have indicated it. There are no such records."

"We've found the skeletons. The Piutes likely got the horses and mules. What about the gold?" said Buck.

"It's probably around here somewhere," said Jerry. "I didn't come in here to find Mormon gold."

Buck flushed a little. "I didn't mean to stop looking for your uncle to find the gold," he said quickly, "but your uncle came into this country looking for that gold. Maybe he found it. Maybe..."

There was no need for Buck to elucidate. Jerry had a quick and clear vision of his uncle's skeleton lying on a pile of gold bullion, like the ghostly *patrons* left by the Spanish miners to protect their cached gold and silver.

"The moon is waning," said Whitey.

"Cheerful place to spend the night," said Buck.

Scat suddenly growled. Whitey dropped to one knee and closed his hand about the dog's muzzle. "Quiet," he hissed.

Buck looked up at the canyon rim. He motioned to Jerry and Whitey to take cover in the thick brush. It was then that Jerry looked up to see three men walking along the canyon rim, sharply silhouetted in the clear moonlight. As he looked, one of them turned so that the moonlight was full on his face. It was Webb Macklin. Somehow the three men had found another way to reach Lost Canyon. The moonlight glinted on a rifle barrel.

Jerry led the way back through the tangle of boulders and brush until the three of them were around a bend in the canyon, in the opposite way from that which the three men were moving.

"We'd better get out of here," said Whitey.

"Why?" said Buck. "They haven't seen us."

"That's right," said Jerry. "Besides, I'm going to take another look in those cliff dwellings." He started up the slope, hearing the others follow him.

It was only a matter of minutes before the moon would be gone. Jerry walked back to the rear corridor behind the dwellings and followed the corridor to the left this time instead of to the right. Here the natural corridor widened greatly and, at the far end of it, the dark mouth of a cave showed. Jerry looked back to see if his two friends were behind him, and as he did so, he could have sworn he saw a faint movement near the cave. He turned quickly and flicked his light toward it. Shadows, in all probability, he thought.

It was then that Scat stopped short and growled. He was staring toward that dark cave mouth.

"Varmint maybe?" said Buck softly.

Jerry had stopped walking. An uneasiness swept through him. In a sense he did not want to enter that dark place just ahead of him, but something compelled him to walk toward it as silently as possible. He knew Buck and Whitey were a few feet behind him, and he wished they were on either side of him, but pride would not let him ask them. Despite Buck's size and strength and Whitey's brains, Jerry was still the leader of the trio, whether he liked the idea or not.

He stopped just outside the cave. A cool, dank draft swept from it, but something else seemed to mingle with it, a faint, though pungent odor, as though something living was in the habit of using the cave for its lair.

Jerry turned the flashlight. The strong beam bored into the darkness, showing a rough rock face ten feet ahead. He walked softly into the cave. Potsherds cracked dryly beneath his boot soles. No one had been in there for centuries. It was all his imagination, but try as he would, he could not discard the thought from his mind.

He reached the rock face, then turned to see if Buck and Whitey were close behind him. As he turned, the rays of the flashlight flicked across the rock wall, revealing deep niches cut into the living rock. The beam glistened on something piled neatly in the niches, like small golden loaves, freshly baked, lying there to cool.

"Lord Almighty," gasped Whitey. "It's gold! Bullion!"

Some sixth sense warned Jerry. He turned quickly, raising his flashlight and the bright light struck a bearded face that seemed to move, silently and disembodied, from the thick darkness of the inner cave. The eyes were wide and glittering in the thin, emaciated face, and a vivid scar on the left temple seemed to stand out like a thick worm beneath the taut flesh covering the skull. He had seen that face before. Then something dark swept through the path of the light and struck Jerry's forearm. The torch clattered to the floor and rolled so that it still shone on the rock face, leaving the rest of the cave in darkness. An eerie shrieking cry echoed from the walls.

A fist skidded across Jerry's forehead. "Look out, fellas!" he screamed as he went low and swung hard with a right and then a left, striking a lean body in the darkness. The strong stench of an unwashed body and filthy clothing swept across Jerry in a sickening miasma.

Scat barked savagely. A big body brushed past Jerry as Buck Lyon joined the fray. He grunted in savage pain as the club bounced from his shoulder. Whitey yelled in fright and anger and dived into the melee. A moment later a hard fist smashed against his jaw and dumped him on top of Scat.

The club swished over Jerry's head. Jerry lowered a

shoulder and hit the man in the gut, driving him back against Buck who wrapped his arms about the screaming opponent. Jerry snatched up the flashlight and shone the light full in the man's staring eyes just as he broke loose from Buck. There was no time to think although, at the very instant Jerry swung the heavy flashlight, he seemed to recognize something startlingly familiar in the contorted features of the man. The blow caught the man alongside the skull and drove him to the floor where one hundred and eighty pounds of hard-muscled football player landed atop him. Buck gripped the thin body, then looked up at Jerry, breathing hard, with sweat glistening from his face. "He's out cold," he said shakily.

"Another minute and I'da had him," said Whitey. He touched his bruised jaw. "Man, what a wallop he had for a guy as hungry looking as he is."

"Who is he?" said Buck. He looked quickly at Jerry.

Jerry handed the flashlight to Buck. The pool of light fell on the bearded face. Jerry's heart thumped like a tom-tom as he eyed the gaunt features, covered with black wiry hair. He was almost sure, and yet...then he remembered something. He ripped back the stained left sleeve of the unconscious man and looked at the wrist. A three-turreted castle had been tattooed on the wrist, symbol of the Engineer Corps of the United States Army. Tears filled his eyes. He looked away from the searching eyes of his two friends. "It's *him* all right," he said in a broken voice. "*My uncle Chuck.*"

"It's a miracle," said Whitey in an awed voice.

"Why did he attack us?" asked Buck. "Maybe he was crazed or something, hey? Man, that *sound* he made! It was enough to give me the cold shakes."

"That must have been him we heard making that cry," said Whitey.

Jerry examined the livid scar on his uncle's forehead. Beside it was the ridged lump he had raised with the heavy flashlight, so close that the two of them seemed one. "I never saw that scar on him," he said. He looked at his two friends. "Do you suppose he had a bad fall somewhere in these canyons, and it wiped out his memory, leaving him to live here like a mad hermit?"

"You've probably hit it," said Buck quietly. "No wonder he never came back."

"But he found what he was looking for," said Whitey.

"Yeh," said Buck. He flicked the light at the gold. "Which reminds me," he added. "We've got three little friends wandering around on the rim of the canyon. Maybe they heard the ruckus. They could hardly miss it if they were within earshot."

Jerry took the flashlight and walked deeper into the cave while Whitey flicked on his smaller light. Piled in a corner was a tangled heap of dried grass, rags, and filthy-looking animal skins. Tin cans and bones littered the floor. A large rusty can was half full of water. He carried the water back to the outer cave and began to bathe his uncle's face. "He lived like an animal," he said quietly, "guarding the gold. Maybe he didn't even know why, but his training and instincts kept him alive."

Buck picked up the hardwood club Charles Hunter had wielded in the short but violent fight. "I'll take a looksee out in the canyon," he said. He disappeared into the darkness of the outer cave.

Whitey eyed the gold bullion. "You think there's a hundred thousand dollars in gold there?"

"I wouldn't doubt it," said Jerry. He wasn't much interested.

"Looks like less than that to me, but then gold is pretty heavy. Kinda heavy for us to take out of here now, being as how we have to help your uncle back to the boat. He comes first."

Jerry nodded. "We'll have to get him out of here when it's dark. If he makes any noise…"

"We can tie him up and gag him. I don't like the idea, but I don't know how else we can manage it. We could leave him here and go for help. One of us could stay here with him."

"No. We'll have to take our chances in getting him out of here tonight, and to the boat well before daylight."

"Supposing *they* got their boat in the same cove?"

Jerry looked up at his friend. "I'm getting my uncle home," he said quietly. "No one is going to stop me. *No one.*

"You have any ideas on how we can hide this gold?"

Jerry saw his uncle's eyelids move. He wet the cloth again and bathed the thin face. Charles Hunter's head moved from side to side. His mouth opened a little.

"I'll take care of it," said Whitey suddenly. He picked up several of the bullion bricks and carried them from the cave. Back and forth he went until the cave was empty of the gold. When he came back, he had a grin on his dusty face. "You know," he said, "if I wasn't me, I'd hate myself for the things I sometimes do."

Jerry ignored his friend. He raised his uncle's head a little. The eyes opened and studied Jerry, and the madness that had been in them was gone. "Hello, kid," said Chuck Hunter. "Long time no see…"

Buck came swiftly into the cave. "We'll have to beat it out of here," he said. "The moon is low, but there's still enough light for them to see us. They're working back up the canyon, fellas. They made it to the bottom. It's only a matter of minutes before they come this way and see the ruins, and they won't likely give them a casual glance as they pass by."

Jerry helped his uncle to his feet. Chuck Hunter looked curiously at Whitey and Buck. "How'd you boys happen to be in here? You look different to me. Bigger and older." He grinned. "Say, Whitey, who clouted you on the jaw?"

"Listen to him," said Whitey under his breath.

"We haven't time to talk," said Jerry. "We've got to get out of here. Now! *Pronto! Andale!*" He gripped his uncle by the arm. "Are you all right? Can you walk?"

"I can out walk, out jump and out spit all three of you put together!"

"Sounds like old Homecoming Week," said Buck dryly.

It didn't take the boys very long to shove some of the more obvious signs of occupancy down a deep crevice at the rear of the cave. Chuck Hunter went along docilely. He knew something was wrong. He also knew he was in good hands.

They left the ruins, working their way down the tangled slope as quietly as they could. The moon was still lighting the upper parts of the ruins, although the Boor of the canyon was black in deep shadow.

They were rounding the bend in the canyon when they heard voices echoing behind them as the three men saw the ruins. Their exploration would take time. Perhaps time enough for the three boys and their charge, Chuck Hunter, to reach the boat. Perhaps...

Chapter 15

A Stern Chase Is a Lang Chase

JERRY HUNTER PEERED DOWN THE LADDER HOLE as Buck Lyon helped Charles Hunter down to the water hole area. Whitey was peering back up the darkening canyon. "Man, oh, man," he said quietly, "if they hear us."

"Get down the hole," said Jerry. "I'll lower Scat."

Whitey scuttled down the shaky ladder. Jerry rigged a sling for Scat. He started to lower the dog into the hole. Scat swung about and his head struck the side of the hole. He barked sharply and through some freak of acoustics, the sound was magnified far out of proportion, echoing clearly through the canyon.

"Oh Lord," said Whitey. He caught the dog and pulled the rope down to the bottom of the hole. "Come on, Jerry! Time's a-wastin'."

Jerry looked back over his shoulder. He sensed, rather than saw or heard, someone in the darkness where the canyon curved toward the cliff dwellings. They could hardly have missed hearing Scat. Jerry pulled some brush about the mouth of the hole. He went down the first ladder and pulled it down after him, lowering it to Whitey, then did the same with the second ladder after he reached the bottom of the lower ladder. The three men in the canyon likely had ropes, and if they did, they'd hardly be much delayed in lowering themselves down to the water hole. The few minutes might make all the difference though.

Jerry and Whitey waded through the pool and saw the dim figures of the other two beside the water's edge. Buck was bent over Charles Hunter. He looked up. "He's weak," he said quietly. "He slipped at the edge of the pool and wrenched his ankle."

"That's all we need," groaned Whitey.

Jerry and Buck took Chuck Hunter up between them. His bearded face was dewed with cold sweat. "Been up and down those crazy ladders hundreds of times," he said, "never fell. Now look at me. Maybe you boys ought to leave me here and go for help."

There was no need to answer him. It was hard work getting him through the narrow and darkened rock passageway into the bigger canyon beyond. There was still enough reflected light in the huge trough for them to be able to pick their way along with some ease, but burdened as they were with the weak and injured man, it was no sinecure.

They had reached the end of the canyon, prepared to leave it for the still larger canyon beyond, when Jerry called a halt. He kneeled beside his uncle and bound the injured ankle tightly with strips of cloth. He looked up. "Better?" he said.

Chuck Hunter nodded. "It's still a long way to the river."

Jerry smiled. "We'll make it," he said.

Scat turned and growled. Above the faint noise of the

rising wind came the distant, muted sound of men's voices. There was little doubt as to who *they* were.

Buck, Whitey, and Jerry stared toward the unseen far end of the canyon. Fear was riding the rising wind.

"Don't panic," said the sharp, incisive voice behind them.

They turned quickly.

Chuck Hunter stood up, leaning on the staff Buck had cut for him. "They're only men," he said. "Let's go!"

There are some men who arc born commanders, whose voices and actions can hold other men when everything else has failed.

The little party moved out into the great canyon that led in its devious passage down to the Colorado and *Huntress*. Try as they would, there was no way of walking quietly. Only the steady keening of the wind might conceal the noise of their passage from those who followed them.

Thick darkness, filled with the noise of the wind, hung over the canyon country. Visibility was limited to twenty or thirty feet. Sweat dripped from their faces as they forced their way on.

"They're having just as hard a time as we are," said Chuck Hunter.

It was Jerry who first noticed the smell of the river. His spirits rose, but then he remembered they had still to get the boat out from under the ledge, get Chuck Hunter into it, and leave the cove before their pursuers reached the river. There was hardly enough time for that. If they knew their quarry was just ahead of them, they'd push on as fast as they could go, forcing the pace, while the three boys were encumbered with Chuck Hunter.

"Evidently they didn't find the bullion," said Buck. "If they had, they'd still be back there gloating over it."

"They couldn't find it," said Whitey. He chuckled.

"Maybe you should have let them have it," said Chuck Hunter. "They'd have left us alone then."

"I wouldn't give them a red cent," said Buck. His slow temper was beginning to smolder.

"Me neither," said Whitey.

Chuck laughed softly. "And I thought it was me who was 'lost treasure' loco," he said.

All the same, thought Jerry, *his uncle was probably right*. If the three men caught up with them, they'd give Uncle Chuck a rough time to find that gold. He was in no condition to be pushed around.

They reached the shore of the cove. Buck waded into the water after pulling off his boots, trousers, and shirt. He swam out to the ledge in the thick darkness.

Whitey backtracked a little up the canyon with Scat to stand watch. It took guts to stand there in that thick, windy darkness, unarmed and alone, waiting for three armed men to show up.

There was no sound from Buck. Jerry waded into the water after he pulled off his boots and trousers. "Buck," he called softly.

No sound but the keening of the wind, the rippling of the disturbed water, the lapping of it on the shore.

"Buck?" called Jerry. Cold fear crept through him. The big kid had been as tired as the rest of them.

"Jerry!" said Buck out of the darkness.

There was something in his voice that frightened Jerry. He waded out and began to swim and then he saw Buck's white face. Something streaked it. When he reached Buck, he saw that it was blood.

"Came up under the ledge," said Buck. "Cut the boat loose. Tried to get in and it smashed me against the rock. Nearly knocked me cold. Boat drifting. Get after it."

"You come first," said Jerry.

Buck grinned weakly. "I can make it," he said. "Good luck."

Jerry slowly breast stroked out into the cove. Visibility was practically nil, close as he was to the choppy surface of the dark waters. Suddenly he saw something looming up in the dimness ahead of him and at the instant he thought it might be *Huntress*. His right foot struck rock with painful force and he was just able to throw up an arm to protect his face from being bashed against wet and naked rock inches in front of him. His foot ached as he swam slowly along the rock face toward the mouth of the cove. There was no sign of the boat. He fended off a small mat of driftwood and saw thicker darkness ahead of him, and before he realized it, he was in the mouth of the cove, and he could hear the subdued rushing of the great river beyond the rock arms of the cove mouth. Something white dimly showed fifty feet ahead of him and his heart seemed to leap as he stroked wearily toward it. Foot by foot he crept toward the drifting boat, gaining steadily, and then it seemed as though the boat was held cupped in a gigantic invisible hand that was drawing it out into the wide river.

He struggled on, spitting out water. It was getting rougher and then with sickening realization he knew he was caught in the firm and relentless watery grasp of the Colorado itself. There was no sense in fighting that liquid muscle and brawn. *Huntress* swirled about in an eddy and a moment later Jerry was in it too, following the boat around and around as though circling the rim of a shallow watery saucer. He tried to cut across the eddy to reach the boat but as he reached the middle of it, he plowed into a tangle of gnarled branches thrust lip from a drifting log, as though the insensate wood were trying to hold him fast like the trees in an enchanted forest.

Huntress was beyond the eddy when at last he freed himself from the slimy grasp of the branches. He hung onto the log and found that he was moving faster that way, due to the great weight of the water-soaked wood. A freak in the current swung the boat about and it seemed to hesitate, as though waiting impatiently for Jerry. The log swirled past her stern, and he let go of it, striking out desperately for the boat, only to see it move away from him, as though with true feminine coquettishness she wanted him to know she wasn't quite ready for his reception.

Jerry sank and went below the turbid surface, taking in a mouthful of the salty water. Fear filled his soul. He panicked and swam with his last reserve of strength toward the dark surface. His head bumped something with sickening force and as his senses whirled, he felt something wet, limp and clinging across his face. He had the presence of mind to grab at it, half expecting to feel the cold, scaly body of a drowned snake, but instead he felt the welcome coldness of wet nylon. He had the bow painter in his hands. He pulled himself close to the boat and tried to board her, but her bow freeboard was high and wet, and he was weakening too fast. With a last surge of his strength, he pulled himself up and gripped a foredeck cleat with his left hand, then got a leg up onto the deck and pulled himself onto the surface of the deck. He lay there breathing hard, with his senses swirling like a maelstrom.

When he managed to drag himself into the cockpit, he knew he was somewhere downstream from the cove, about in the middle of the rushing river, with nothing to guide him. He staggered to the controls and put the mono control into neutral, advancing the hand throttle. He walked back to the motor and kneeled to grip the primer tube on the fuel line. He squeezed it until he could feel the pressure built up in the line. He stood up and pulled out the choke, then gripped the starter handle. He pulled it until he felt the ratchet mechanism engaged, then pulled vigorously. Nothing happened. He tried it again, then remembered to check to see if the fuel line was kinked. It was. He straightened it, then pumped the primer tube again to build up the pressure. He pulled the starter again and the motor coughed and spluttered, then died away.

Wearily he checked everything once more, then pulled the starter. She coughed, spluttered, coughed again, then started to hum erratically. He pushed down on the choke, then made his way forward to the controls. He eased off the hand throttle, then pushed forward the mono control until the boat began to move under her own power. It was as dark as the inside of a boot on the wide river hemmed in by sheer and towering cliffs. He slowly turned her about against the powerful current and moved upstream, staring at the dark shoreline for a sign of the cove. It all looked alike over there. There were many such coves. The throbbing of the motor boomed back and forth in the dark canyon. Anyone within a mile could hear it.

He took a desperate chance, poking in close to the shore, hoping he wouldn't snag the hull on a pinnacle of rock or smash into driftwood. It was no use, he couldn't differentiate one cove from another. He looked back over his shoulder, praying for a sign. It was then that he saw the shielded flashlight beam flick off and on three times, not two hundred yards from him, there was no time to waste. He steered directly toward it at cruising speed, trusting to sheer luck. Something bumped against the hull but he kept on. He entered the cove and throttled back, letting her move slowly toward the shore. The light flicked on once more and a few minutes later the bow grated solidly on the shingle.

Buck splashed into the water and turned to give Chuck Hunter a hand into the boat. Jerry's uncle fell weakly into the bottom. "Looks familiar," he said wryly.

"Whitey!" called Buck.

"Coming! So is someone else!"

Scat barked. Buck scooped him up and dumped him on top of Chuck Hunter. Whitey gripped the bow and with the help of Buck, they shoved the boat back into the deeper water. Whitey scrambled aboard.

"Halt there!" a man yelled. "Halt or we shoot!"

Jerry threw the motor into reverse and turned the wheel. Whitey fell heavily into the bottom of the boat. Men were yelling on the dark shore. Jerry gunned the big motor and shot toward the mouth of the cove. A gun cracked flatly, and something hummed just over Jerry's head.

"There's their boat!" said Buck.

Jerry saw it too, at the far right-hand side of the cove, just distinguishable in the darkness.

"We got time to disable it?" said Buck.

A gun flatted off again and the plastic windshield of the fleeing boat shattered in the center.

"There's your answer," said Jerry. He crouched low and gave *Huntress* all the power she could take. She leaped forward like a thing alive and shot past the right-hand side of the cove mouth with inches to spare.

Once more a gun cracked but *Huntress* had reached the river channel by now. Jerry turned her downstream and she bucked and almost leaped across a wide eddy, shunted aside a piece of driftwood and reached the middle of the dark channel. It would be but a matter of minutes for those three men back there to reach their boat, start both motors and surge out into the river in full hue and cry after the slower *Huntress*.

The wind was still rising, moaning down the canyon, lifting the surface water into a tossing froth. It would be a rough night on the more open water. The red storm signals would be flying down at the Lower Basin.

Huntress rounded a dark and looming island. Ahead in the darkness Jerry saw a channel light indicating a sharp turn to port past the mouth of Grand Wash. As the boat turned into the channel leading out of Grand Wash Canyon Buck slapped Jerry on the shoulder. Jerry turned. Coming up behind them were the swiftly moving lights of another boat. There wasn't any doubt in his mind about who would be racing like that.

"Maybe we should hide somewhere?" said Whitey. "It's a long way to the end of Lower Basin."

"You can't hide from bullets," said Buck.

"We've got a fair lead," said Jerry. "It will take a faster boat than theirs to overcome the lead we've got. For a time at least."

"You can't outrace bullets," said Whitey.

"It will take a good man to hit us from a bouncing boat in this light," said Buck.

"Keep going, kid," said Chuck Hunter. "We're not licked yet."

Jerry was tired and his mind was confused, not quite the conditions he would have wanted in a chase such as this. In all likelihood the river would be deserted. Such a wind would drive all boats into sheltered coves, and those back in the Lower Basin would not leave the safety of their moorings once the storm flags were flying. There were miles and miles of dark river channel ahead of *Huntress* which was being pursued by a faster boat, with armed and desperate men in her. If Jerry took a chance and tried to hide the boat in a cove, they might succeed, for a time at least, in giving their pursuers the slip, but once *Huntress* was committed to the run downriver, there was little chance of going anywhere else.

"A stem chase is a long chase," said Chuck Hunter.

They raced across the choppy waters, with the wide mouth of Grand Wash to starboard. Iceberg Canyon would open in the thick darkness about three miles ahead of them. Meanwhile there were no turns in the channel to protect them from gunfire.

Jerry pushed the throttle further forward and *Huntress* planed like a gull, slapping the waves with her bottom, sending up sheets of spray. The pounding was getting heavy, and it wouldn't help her hull, but they had no choice. Buck slipped a poncho about Jerry's shoulders. Spray flicked over the windshield and when the boat wallowed, trying to recover, some of it slopped over the sides.

At Jerry's command, the others moved about in the boat to place their weight in the best positions. Scat, who weighed all of twenty pounds, worked his way past Jerry's legs into the shelter of the area below the fore-deck, curling in a ball atop a bunk. A short way out into the more open waters of the Grand Wash area convinced Jerry that they were in for a rough and wet ride. He looked back to see the oncoming lights. They hadn't gained much, if any.

"Imagine how it's going to be in Virgin Basin and Lower Basin," said Buck.

"If we get that far," said Whitey gloomily.

Jerry picked up the lights of the channel into Iceberg

Canyon and they seemed a long way off across those rough, dark waters. Another thought came into his mind. At the speed he was pushing the boat, the fuel supply would dwindle far too fast for safety. There might be enough in the reserve to make the marina at Lower Basin.

They held their lead into Iceberg Canyon and the roaring of the fifty-horsepower motor mingled with the moaning of the wind through the high-walled gorge. A quarter of the way into the canyon and the lights showed up astern, still in about the same relative position. They weren't gaining, nor were they losing. In a flat, outright run, on sheltered waters, they'd close the gap to a perilous distance. On the open, rougher waters. *Huntress* had a better chance of keeping ahead, but probably at the cost of a racked hull. If she started to take on water, the increased weight might make the difference in winning or losing the desperate race.

They picked up the light on huge Sandy Point and in a matter of minutes they were surging down Gregg Basin at full speed, getting a small taste of what they could expect in the more open waters of the bigger basins. *Huntress* would yaw from side to side in the grip of waves and water, wallowing deeply, throwing up sheets of spray, soaking everything in the cockpit.

Chuck Hunter moved up into the seat beside Jerry. "She's pure thoroughbred," he said quietly.

"Do you think we can out race them?" asked Jerry.

"Hard to say. We can take a chance on ducking into Temple Bar Landing. There will likely be quite a few people there. Protection in numbers, you know."

Buck wiped spray from his face. "I'll buy that," he agreed.

Jerry looked back, and something came quickly into

his mind. Something about Sandy Point that might work to their advantage. He turned the wheel a little, moving out of the center of the channel, heading for Sandy Point. His uncle looked quizzically at him.

"They're gaining a little," said Buck.

Huntress was full out now, straining for the tip of the point. Beyond the tip were some small coves, hardly shelter against those who were slowly closing the gap behind *Huntress*.

"You'll lose ground cutting out of the channel," said Whitey anxiously.

Jerry did not speak. Slowly he eased back on the throttle.

"Motor trouble, Jerry?" demanded Buck.

Jerry shook his head. He looked back at the oncoming lights. The other boat was rapidly closing the gap, planing at great speed through the darkness, revealed by the flying sheets of spray. He looked ahead. He was nearing the point. The waters were shallower here and shoaled quickly close under the point.

The other boat was no more than a hundred yards behind *Huntress* now, bounding almost triumphantly at great speed, stern low in the water, twin rooster tails flying behind her swiftly revolving propellers.

Jerry looked ahead. There was a patch of darker water, or what at least *looked* like darker water. The gamble was his to take. He turned the wheel, heading inshore.

"He's gone loco!" snapped Buck.

The other boat turned too. Jerry moved alongside the darker patch of water, then suddenly shoved forward the mono control, setting *Huntress* low in the stern as she roared ahead, rounding sharply, throwing up spray. Jerry thanked God that Whitey had thought of those stabilizers, for otherwise he might have swamped *Huntress*. He turned her sharply again to clear the darker patch of water and as he did so he looked back. Even above the roaring of the three motors he heard the hard, thudding smash of wood against wood, and the lights flicked out as though extinguished by a giant, invisible snuffer. It was the signal for Jerry to ram the mono control fully forward. *Huntress* squatted low in the water for a few seconds, then leaped up to plane like a gull heading for the center of the channel, with Sandy Point looming close to port.

Chuck Hunter stared back through the darkness. "I don't get it," he said.

Jerry grinned. "I remembered there was a big eddy back there, where the river floats in brush and driftwood. It's always turning about in the area back there. That was that darker patch of water you saw. I skirted it, figuring they might not know it was there. *They didn't.*"

They reached the river center and before they rounded Sandy Point for the rest of the run down Gregg Basin, they all looked back. There was no sign of the other boat. No lights glinting from the dark waters.

Chuck Hunter patted Jerry on the shoulder. "Kid," he said, "Remind me never to try to outfox you."

"Let me take the wheel," said Buck. "Get some rest, Jerry."

Even so, as Jerry left the wheel and squatted in the stern beside Whitey, he looked thoughtfully back toward Sandy Point. The night was long, and so were the miles to Lower Basin.

Chapter 16

"Huntress" Shows Her Heels

THEY HAD TAKEN TIME TO REPLENISH THE TANK from the reserve fuel supply as they moved steadily down Gregg Basin. In the six miles or so since they had left Sandy Point behind, they had not seen the lights of another boat behind them. Buck drove the boat into Virgin Canyon, and it was as dark as the lobby to Hades, with the sound of the motor booming back and forth between the canyon walls. They were bucking a rising head wind as they moved westerly through the canyon, which would mean trouble later on in Virgin and Lower Basins.

Five more watery miles were behind them when they reached the western end of Virgin Canyon, passing Salt Springs Wash to port. Whitey was sound asleep, cuddled up with Scat on one of the bunks, while Chuck Hunter occupied the other bunk. Jerry sat behind Buck, watching astern, while Buck drove steadily on through the night. He turned as they passed the light at the base of Temple Mesa.

"Temple Bar Landing?" he queried.

"I think so. There are bound to be others there. Maybe even a Ranger or two. Maybe they aren't following us, but I don't want to take any chances with Uncle Chuck."

"I wish we could make more speed, but it's getting windier and much rougher. I'm glad we don't have to face Virgin and Lower Basins this night."

Almost as though echoing his words, the motor skipped a beat or two, roared on, then coughed several times. Jerry hurried back to it. The motor was missing steadily.

"What do you think, Jerry?" asked Buck.

"Water in the gas maybe."

"Shall we stop?"

"Keep going. She might work through it."

"If they came up on us now, we'd never get away from them."

"I haven't seen them," said Jerry.

There was nothing to do but keep on, at exasperatingly low speed, moving out into the more open water beyond the projecting rock formation called the Temple. The full force of the open water caught them as they rounded slowly to head for Temple Bar Landing. The motor sounded worse instead of better and they began to lose their way.

Buck idled the motor. Suddenly it cut out. Jerry gripped the starter handle and pulled at it several times until the motor caught again. They might have to clean the water out of the line and the tank, but it would take half an hour to forty-five minutes. They had little choice but to head into Temple Bar Landing. It was dark and windy, and the distant lights seemed to taunt them as the boat pitched up and down on the water.

The motor seemed to run a little better. Jerry slapped

it. "Come on," he coaxed. "Come on, baby!" It was then that he looked back to see the lights of a boat coming up fast astern and his heart sank within him. The motor coughed, almost died, caught again, then roared on. Meanwhile the other boat was cutting inside of them to get between them and Temple Bar Landing. The way *Huntress'* motor was acting, they didn't have much to worry about. *Huntress* couldn't outrun a rowboat right now.

The motor caught and missed, caught and missed, losing precious seconds for the boat. There was no chance to cut into Temple Bar Landing now. Then the motor caught on full throatily and *Huntress* leaped forward, slapping into the choppy waters. They couldn't make Temple Bar Landing. There was nothing to do but run as fast as they could up the channel that led to Virgin Basin, despite the pounding the boat would take.

The lead over the following boat was just about the same as it had been before Jerry had decoyed them into the driftwood back at Sandy Point. It had delayed them, but it hadn't stopped them.

Chuck Hunter came out into the cockpit and looked grimly back at the pursuing boat. He looked infinitely weary. "No chance to get into Temple Bar Landing?" he said quietly.

"If we can get out into Virgin Basin we might have a chance," said Buck. "It won't help *Huntress* any."

"It's a chance we'll have to take," said Jerry. "Just don't drive her under, Buck."

Huntress was doing her best as she fled toward Virgin Basin five miles away. The wind was funneling into the channel. The flashing red light near the Campanile flicked past in the windy darkness. Ahead of them was East Point, marked by a flashing white light, and beyond that was the rough open water of the basin, fully nine to ten miles across to the flashing white light that marked the eastern entrance to Boulder Canyon.

Before they even reached Virgin Basin, the coming storm showed its latent fury. Wind and water tore at the racing boat. Every time Buck throttled back to ease her, the oncoming lights grew steadily larger. They were forcing the bigger, more powerful boat, knowing they could take far more punishment than *Huntress*.

Water was sloshing back and forth in the bilge. Jerry aroused Whitey and they began to bail out die boat but, it seemed, as fast as they threw it out, more came in. Jerry had the cold feeling that they had started a seam somewhere and that was why she was taking so much water. It surely couldn't be from spray alone. He did not dare speak his fears. Once they hit the open water of the Virgin Basin the water slowly began to gain.

Whitey looked at Jerry. "Seam?" he asked softly.

"Don't know." Jerry looked back. "I think we had better lighten ship."

Overboard went everything they did not need, sleeping bags, food hampers, empty thermos jugs, camping equipment and canned food. *Huntress* seemed to ride a little easier, but the water was still coming in. Now all three of them, Chuck, Whitey, and Jerry were heaving water over the side.

Sometimes the other boat would draw closer, then *Huntress* would pull ahead, but she was taking a terrible beating. A less well-built boat would have filled and swamped by now. There were no other lights on the dark, heaving waters of the basin, beyond the navigation lights and the lights of the pursuing boat. Now and then *Huntress* would dip deeply, until it seemed she wasn't going to come up, but somehow she managed it, boring into the tumbling waters, scattering spray high to either side of her sleek bows.

The motor showed no evidence of the trouble it had had awhile back. If it happened again... Jerry cast the thought from his mind. They had a chance of staying ahead, rough as the open water was, but once inside Boulder Canyon, about five miles long, fairly well sheltered from the wind, the power the other boat had might make the difference in the wild race.

There was nothing to do but hang on, bail, and pray.

The night seemed darker than ever, and the wind was howling madly across the desert and mountain country, beating viciously at Lake Mead with its invisible flail. Even the most powerful and biggest of boats on the lake would not have attempted a crossing of Virgin Basin that mad night, and Lower Basin had a worse reputation than Virgin Basin when the wind came from that direction.

Closer and closer appeared the flashing white light at the dark entrance to Boulder Canyon, beyond which was the Lower Basin. It seemed to Jerry that *Huntress* was plowing doggedly through a sea of viscous mud that didn't seem to bother the boat astern of them. In the more sheltered waters of the canyon the pursuing boat might very well catch up with them. There would be no one to see the results. It would be simple enough for them to come alongside and hold the three boys at gunpoint while they took Chuck Hunter into their boat. After that? Simple and deadly. Sink *Huntress* many fathoms deep and make sure the boys did not reach shore. No bullet holes, of course; that would be too incriminating if any of the bodies washed ashore. Just sink the boat and drift while three tired boys struck out for the distant and unseen shore. One by one they'd go under, or be *helped* under.

"No chance to hole up?" said Whitey.

"No," said Buck. "We're not far enough ahead of them."

The flashing white light was passed, and the roaring of the hard-pressed motor mingled with the dervish howling of the wind in the high-walled canyon. The water was smoother and Buck drove at top speed. *Huntress* stopped taking in as much water.

"We could leave the boat one by one and swim ashore," suggested Whitey. "Let *Huntress* go on."

Jerry was tired. He knew Buck was suffering far more from the blow he had received on his head than he had let on. Certainly Chuck Hunter lacked the strength to buck his way ashore, even in the smoother waters of the canyon. Whitey was hardly a good enough swimmer to make it, and he too was tired from previous exertions and lack of sleep.

"We've got to make the marina," said Buck.

Huntress seemed to respond as she planed and leaped through the narrow entrance of the canyon, then past Wishing Well Cove and James Bay, with no chance to cut into one of them for shelter. At the far end of the widest part of the canyon the lights of the pursuing boat appeared and she was making up lost time. Beyond a sharp right-hand turn the lights were lost and then as *Huntress* roared into the last stretch of the canyon the lights appeared again, closer this time.

They could see the flashing lights on either shore, green to starboard, red to port, as they rounded into the beginning area of the Lower Basin. Then the flashing white light on Beacon Island appeared through the windy darkness. Now and then Buck's head sagged forward until at last Jerry slid into the seat beside him and tapped him on the shoulder. Buck nodded, then stepped over the back of the seat to drop into the bottom of the wet cockpit. His face was drawn and white and dried blood showed on his hairline.

Jerry got the feel of the boat and the water. It wasn't quite as rough as he had expected, but they had not reached the more open waters of the basin and they had a long run of at least ten miles to reach the marina. He looked back. The other boat was not yet in sight.

Past Beacon Island, as Callville Bay opened up far to starboard and seemed to let out a Boreas bagful of howling wind. *Huntress* began to wallow and pitch in the clutch of the water. Jerry could hear the bailing cans rattling on the bottom of the boat. Water streamed through the cracked windshield, shattered by the bullet. If the other boat closed the gap sufficiently, there would be more bullets whispering through the darkness.

"Bout time for the Yewnited States Guard to show up, flags flying, guns spitting flame and smoke, to board those pirates, ain't it?" said Whitey. "Like in the movies?"

"They've got enough sense to stay off this lake tonight," grunted Buck.

Jerry looked back. His uncle was sprawled in the bottom of the pitching, heaving boat, feebly trying to bail, but most of the time the can rattled emptily. Despair flew silently overhead on velvety wings, looking for a perch to land upon in the boat below.

Whitey's face was a sickly greenish white. His bailing can fell from his grasp, and he thrust his head over the side of the boat to commune with the dashing waves.

There was no choice for Jerry but to smash the boat almost headlong into the pitching waters. He dared a glance astern, and his heart seemed to sink within him. The gap was slowly closing. Halfway down the basin the gap would be narrow enough for them to start shooting. No other boat lights showed on the dark waters.

When at last he saw the distant flashing green light on Black Island, far to starboard, he knew he had at least a six-mile run to the marina. He looked back. The boat behind them had closed the gap to about two hundred yards. Still too far to shoot with accuracy.

Ten minutes later the gap had closed to one hundred and fifty yards. Jerry looked down at his uncle and friends. "Stay low," he said. "If they start shooting the motor might protect you. Stay low and hang on, no matter what I do!"

Jerry eased back on the mono control. *Huntress* took the seas more kindly. It took all the guts he had to let the boat slow down, knowing they were coming up fast astern, but there was a simple plan in his tired brain, something he had remembered from the day he and his two friends had taken the girls out for a cruise.

He glanced back and his heart quailed. The other boat was no more than seventy-five yards behind them, coming up far too fast, tossing great sheets of spray as she bucked the fury of the lake. Any minute now, he thought. Any minute a chunk of lead might sing past his ear or bury itself in his flesh.

He glanced back again. The gap was now no more than twenty yards, and he could see the grinning face of the man at the wheel, or at least Jerry *thought* he was grinning. Jerry eased back on the throttle. The other boat was coming up too fast. At the last split second, Jerry rammed the mono control forward and swung the wheel hard to starboard, wrenching the boat through a high wave. As he did so he thanked God, *and* Whitey Cramer, for thinking of adding those stabilizers on each side of the hull, for *Huntress* leaped ahead while the other helmsman, caught by surprise, attempted to make the same fast turn. Even above the howling of the wind and the noise of the motors, Jerry could hear them yelling back there.

He looked back. The other boat was wallowing sickeningly in the trough, trying to get up enough speed to follow *Huntress,* and he knew that as long as he could maneuver like that, he could keep up the game for quite a while. He also knew he could never outrace those bullets. If they got tired of his tactics, they could always start shooting. Some of their bullets would strike home.

He eased back on the mono control as the other boat came roaring up close astern. Then he swung *Huntress* hard aport and gunned the motor, slamming at full speed toward the unseen marina while the other, more tender boat, wallowed again in the trough of the waves, trying to get forward speed.

Three times he pulled his maneuver, and each time gained precious seconds and yards. The fourth time, when *Huntress* swung into her hard turn, he heard the flat report of a gun, and something slammed into metal and sang thinly off into the darkness. They were trying to hit the motor. He noticed something else as well. There was the faintest tinge of pearl gray high in the eastern sky, the coming of the false dawn.

The pursuing craft swung close on the course of *Huntress.* "Hang on," said Jerry over his shoulder. He swung *Huntress,* then swung her hard again, almost turning her up on her beam ends, shooting back almost directly at the other boat. He could see the contorted faces of the three men in the boat as they yelled and cursed at him. *Huntress* flicked past, not more than ten yards away, racing in the opposite direction. The big man named Siskin held a revolver in his right hand, steadying his aim by holding his right wrist with his left hand. Webb Macklin was at the wheel. He wrenched it hard, to turn after *Huntress.* Siskin pitched over the side and went under, leaving a piercing scream hanging in the windy air. Macklin did not stop. He shoved forward his twin throttles and surged after *Huntress.* It was evident that he had no intention of going back after Siskin. Jerry knew full well then the manner of men with which they were dealing.

He could see, far ahead, as he turned *Huntress* once again to follow his true course, the faint lights marking the marina. Sentinel Island loomed to port and farther ahead was the flashing red light on the Boulder Islands. Beyond that was the marina, hardly more than two or three miles away from *Huntress* and her crew.

"They're coming up fast again," said Buck.

"So is the water in here," said Whitey quietly.

The bailing cans rattled. *Huntress* was not only taking water through the hull, but a great deal of it was slopping over the side and spraying back from the plunging bows. Jerry's back, bottom and sides were sore from the pounding he was taking as he drove the careening boat. The eastern sky was much lighter now.

Between Sentinel Island and Boulder Islands the pursuing boat made time, closing the gap at a steady pace, while *Huntress,* partly full of water, was losing its precious lead. Jerry looked back. There was one last shot in the locker. A dangerous one, but there was no choice. It was a gamble he had to take or lose the deadly game they had played all night long.

He eased back on the throttle. The boat closed in. He could hear them yelling at *Huntress* to stop and let them come alongside. Closer and closer she came. She was traveling at high, pounding speed. Jerry rammed forward the mono control. The motor coughed, roared, coughed and shuddered, then roared again. He drove at top speed directly for the oncoming boat.

"You playing chicken, you crazy idiot!" roared Buck.

"Shut up and hang on," gritted Jerry.

At the last possible second the other boat seemed to lose its nerve. Macklin jerked back his throttles and slammed them into reverse. The bigger boat shuddered convulsively, then moved back, and just as Jerry had anticipated, a smooth, dark wave flowed high about the twin motors and cascaded into the cockpit. One of the motors coughed into silence. The boat lost way and broached to. Another wave rose greasily up the side as the boat dipped to meet it, then flowed into the cockpit, to be followed by yet another. The second motor sputtered and then died. Moments later the cockpit was full from gunnel to gunnel and two desperate and yelling men were floundering around in the water. "Give us a hand!" screamed Macklin. "You can't let us drown out here!"

Jerry eased the mono control and *Huntress* turned obediently as he moved the wheel. "Throw those guns over the side!" he yelled. "Now! *Pronto! Andale!*"

Two guns splashed into the water. *Huntress* moved easily alongside. The bigger boat was almost fully awash now. The man named Carl stepped over the side and struck out for *Huntress*. Buck pulled him over the side, waved a fist under his nose, and made him fall flat on the bottom of the cockpit, inches deep in bilge water.

Webb Macklin looked about. The boat was sinking under his feet. He stared at the other boat. Then his boat sank from beneath him with a sobbing gurgling sound, as though tired of it all. Macklin struck out. He hooked an arm over the side of *Huntress*. Whitey gave him a hand. As Macklin stepped into the cockpit, he suddenly thrust a hand inside his soaked shirt and yanked out a knife. It was the last sudden movement he'd make for quite some time. A hard left fist sank into his belly and a hard right fist smashed against his down coming chin as he doubled up. Buck Lyon had finally achieved his ambition. He blew thoughtfully on his knuckles and grinned at his friends.

"*Ole!*" said Whitey.

Jerry headed *Huntress* for the marina, easing her along. She had done her duty, and she could be repaired as good as new with time and loving care.

The dawn light began to filter over the heaving waters of the lake. The wind was dying away in fitful gusts and spurts. The white light just off the marina flashed its welcome to a tired boat and a weary crew.

Just as *Huntress* eased into the anchorage the motor died. Jerry looked back at Whitey. Whitey rubbed the gauge atop the tank. "Empty," he said. "Wouldn't you know it!"

Jerry let her drift to the shore. They grounded her. Buck and Whitey worked swiftly lashing the wrists of both prisoners behind them. Chuck Hunter climbed slowly out of the boat. "I don't suppose your mother would mind making breakfast for four hungry mariners, would she, kid?" he said.

Jerry smiled. "I think the best thing we can do right now is go up and ask her."

The sun came up slowly behind the mountains, staining the sky rose and gold, and flooding light into the dark, cold canyons and onto the waters of Lake Mead. It promised to be a fine day.

Chapter 17

Beyond the Colorado

LOST CANYON DREAMED ON IN THE HOT JULY sunlight. The sound of voices echoed from the opening beside the placid upper water hole. A hawk, hanging with outstretched wings against the sharp hot blue of the sky, suddenly banked and let the dry wind carry it over the rim of the canyon. It was a silent world of rock and brush once more until the voices arose in the canyon below the cliff dwellings.

The party stopped at the foot of the talus slope below the dwellings. Eight people studied the silent, brooding ruins. Charles and William Hunter stood together, with Jerry behind them. The others were Buck Lyon and Whitey Cramer, amid a bevy of girls Linda Bedloe, Helene Squires, and Candy Kingman. Scat eyed the ruins with mild interest.

"It's hard to believe," said Bill Hunter at last.

"Are they *real?*" asked Candy.

"You should see them in the moonlight," said Whitey.

"No, thanks," said Candy. She shivered a little despite the clinging heat.

"And that is where you lived for three years, Chuck?" asked Bill Hunter quietly.

Chuck Hunter laughed softly. "As far as I know," he said. "Some of it comes back to me. Much of it is lost forever. I have vague recollections of running along the canyon rims, baying at the moon, when the madness held me."

"Yeh," said Whitey dryly. "So do we."

"I suppose I stayed alive by sheer instinct," said Chuck. "There was plenty of water. Good shelter. Animals aplenty. I rigged snares and deadfalls. I remember once finding a deer with a broken leg. Its meat kept me alive for a long time. Now and then I would walk into one of the towns, Fredonia, maybe Saint George, I don't really remember, and buy food, when the mood came over me. I had some money. It never occurred to me to turn myself in. No one bothered me. There are a lot of oddball characters drifting about this country. Sometimes I stole food from boats I found moored in the coves. I did some fishing." He laughed again. "Not a bad life when you think about it."

"And a rich man to boot," said Buck. "Without knowing it, of course."

"If it's still there," said Chuck. He looked at Whitey.

They started up the slope to the terrace.

"I was being followed by our three cx-friends, Macklin, Siskin, and Carl," continued Chuck. "I hated to do it, but I sank *Explorer* in the cove to hide it from them. I fully expected to return to Boulder City of course, laden with Mormon gold. Somewhere in here I had a bad fall. You all know the rest of the story."

Whitey led the way into the natural tunnel or

corridor at the rear of the dwellings, then turned with a sly look on his face. "Well, here it is," he said triumphantly.

They all looked about. There was nothing to be seen but the crumbling walls and the living rock.

"The kid has finally flipped his wig," said Buck.

Whitey leaned against one of the walls. "That's brawn speaking, not brains," he said casually. He winked at Helene.

Jerry looked about. Whitey couldn't have gone very far the night he had taken the gold from the cave and hidden it. Not much further than from where he was now standing. He eyed the crumbling wall, then he walked over and lifted one of the top bricks. It was surprisingly heavy, and the dust slid from its golden surface as he turned it.

Whitey grinned. One by one he took the bullion bricks from the wall, handing each of them one in turn, then placing one in front of Scat. "Sometimes I hate myself because I'm so sneaky," he said.

"Isn't he cute?" crowed Helene.

Bill Hunter hefted a brick and looked at the other bricks. "Obviously there isn't one hundred thousand dollars' worth here," he said thoughtfully.

"No," said Chuck. "It's enough, though, to satisfy anyone."

"I'll buy that," said Buck.

Chuck hefted his brick. He looked at the others. "Now that I've found it, it doesn't mean much to me," he said quietly. "I think perhaps the Mormon Church could find good use for their long-lost gold, don't you?"

There was no answer. Whitey gulped. "All of it?" he asked in a very small voice.

"All of it," said Chuck Hunter. He grinned. "I have an

idea the church won't forget you boys, for if it hadn't been for the three of you, and Scat here; a bearded madman might still be guarding gold for which he had absolutely no use."

"Amen," said Bill Hunter.

They carried the bricks toward the opening to the terrace.

"What about him, Uncle Chuck?" asked Jerry, pointing to the arrow-pierced skeleton lying in the dusty shadows.

Chuck Hunter tilted his head to one side. "Why disturb him now, kid? The dead rest easy if they are not disturbed. Let him rest in peace. After all, *he has found his tomorrow...*"

They walked down the slope and up the quiet canyon. In a little while their voices died away. The hawk swung back over the canyon on motionless wings. The wind whispered through the dry brush. The cliff dwellings seemed to settle a little as though seeking a softer spot on the rock. Higher and higher in the cobalt sky a milky trail of vapor from a jet stained the blue and the faint sound of the motor died away. It was quiet and peaceful again, beyond the Colorado.

A Look at: Mystery of the Haunted Mine and The Secret of the Spanish Desert

Two Full Length Young Adult Western Mystery Novels

Embark on two full length exhilarating adventures alongside teenagers Gary Cole, Tucker Browne, and Sue Browne as they venture unchartered territories in search of lost fortunes!

In *Mystery of the Haunted Mine*, somewhere tucked away in these canyons is a life-changing treasure...thousands upon thousands of dollars' worth of gold that many a man has searched and died for over the years spanning back as far as their grandfathers' time. The Indians say it is guarded by ghosts, but Gary, Tuck, and Sue refuse to believe that ghosts use live ammunition... Like Perry Mason's triumphs in the courtroom, these determined young adventurers must overcome adversity and emerge unscathed.

During *The Secret of the Spanish Desert*, while exploring the vast desert, Gary stumbles upon an enticing secret—a lost Spanish Mission waiting to be discovered. As the trio unravels the enigmatic tale, they encounter a mysterious spectral figure draped in the robes of a friar—just one of the many perplexing dilemmas that lie ahead for our intrepid sleuths—and their relentless pursuit takes them deeper into the arid wasteland, where danger lurks at every turn.

Join Gary, Tucker, and Sue on two unforgettable journeys, as they face desert-bound obstacles and unmask the secrets buried within. Will you answer the call? Adventure awaits.

AVAILABLE NOW

About the Author

Gordon D. Shirreffs published more than 80 western novels, 20 of them juvenile books, and John Wayne bought his book title, Rio Bravo, during the 1950s for a motion picture, which Shirreffs said constituted *"the most money I ever earned for two words."* Four of his novels were adapted to motion pictures, and he wrote a Playhouse 90 and the Boots and Saddles TV series pilot in 1957.

A former pulp magazine writer, he survived the transition to western novels without undue trauma, earning the admiration of his peers along the way. The novelist saw life a bit cynically from the edge of his funny bone and described himself as looking like a slightly parboiled owl. Despite his multifarious quips, he was dead serious about the writing profession.

Gordon D. Shirreffs was the 1995 recipient of the Owen Wister Award, given by the Western Writers of America for "a living individual who has made an outstanding contribution to the American West."

He passed in 1996.

www.ingramcontent.com/pod-product-compliance
Lightning Source LLC
Chambersburg PA
CBHW021159210626
46816CB00009BA/2618